My Friend Henry

Published by

Percychatteybooks Publishing

ISBN 978 1 9998869 7 4

© Percy W Chattey 2018

My Friend Henry

Story Telling Ten

Percychatteybooks
Five times winner of the
Pinnacle Awards

With love to my wife and best friend Jean. My grateful thanks for all the hours spent putting up with me while I am positioning these words together..

Also my appreciation to:
Derek Cook for the cover design

Other books by the Author

Motorway

Humpty Majority Sat on the Wall

Who called Last Orders

Living in Spain

Politically Incorrect

Blitz & Pieces

The Black Venus

Watchit!

Watchit Too!

Death for a Starter

The Dauntless Factor

The Cormacks

Time Gentlemen

Reign of Terror 1940

Percy's Ramblings

Telling Tales

As a young man grows into adulthood, he learns to accept his friend Henry's desires and how he dominates his life.

My Friend Henry

Chapter One.

One Friday Evening in 1966

It is early evening, and after a late start we are speeding along in a dream of a car from the Longbridge Works near Birmingham. Dennis Walker is my name and with my friend Henry we are looking forward,

with excitement and anticipation, to our arrival at the small cottage by the sea. Who is Henry you may well ask? I'll introduce him to you later in the story, but I can assure you he is my little best friend.

Hopefully, my desires and thoughts are right and when we arrive at our destination, I will be getting very close to the wonderful Sally, the lady sitting beside me. The eagerness and expectation is flowing through me listening to her voice as she sings along to the music from the tape deck fitted to the car.

My Friend Henry

From the cars music centre our favourite melody, carefully chosen, smooth and soft is playing. The gentle light from the control panel, creating a shine on the nylon stockings covering the shapely legs spread out in front of Sally.

As I just said she is singing and humming to the music and is totally relaxed in the comfortable seat as we speed along on our journey in the blue saloon car. Her coloured flared skirt, by chance a similar matching shade as the vehicle, was reaching just below her knees, hiding all sorts of wonders below.

My heart is pounding as I feel the powerful engine surging us forward. With experience I steer to follow the reflection of the glass cat's eyes embedded in the road, replicating the double twin lights from the cars headlights.

We are travelling rapidly on our way West out of London, heading towards the coast, with the reflected light showing in detail the twists and turns of the country lane with its high hedge rows to each side.

Once more, as I had done a number of times during the journey, I glance over at her delightful form, slim waist and a beautiful feminine shape covered in the high neck

My Friend Henry

line of her satiny blouse, with tiny matching buttons running down the centre...oh how I wanted to undo them. Silky shining blond hair cascading down over her shoulders in waves. Her hands were keeping in time with the music with fingers clicking to the rhythm in her lap. She sensed me looking and coyly turned and smiled sweetly back at me, her eyes flashing in some form of promise.

The hum of the tyres and the murmur of the engine as the car propelled us onwards, passing through quaint small villages with twinkling streetlights, otherwise all very quiet and empty with not a sign of anyone being about. Each would look good adorning the front of a post card or chocolate box.

All that is insignificant to us as we are happily involved in each other's company. There is an air of excitement as we each ponder the weekend in front of us, filled for certain with the intimacy of being together. Sally and I both sense the closeness between us, a warm wonderful feeling enhanced by the delicate perfume she is wearing.

A sensation of wanting to be together, pulled by some invisible magic. A feeling of a deep love developing between us as we sing along to the music. My own hands were trembling slightly at the thought of arriving at our destination. I could feel the blood pumping through me at the thought of being close together, but was I expecting too much?

Chapter Two

A Pair of Laughing Eyes

It has now been almost two years since my life changed, up to now very much for the better. At that time it had been a normal week with the usual amount of problems in my work of selling cars, mainly trying to explain to customers the inner working of vehicles and watching the blank look on their faces, instantly knowing they had no idea what I was talking about.

I worked for a large Company as a senior salesperson, which really meant my life was my own although I did have to answer to a manager, but on the whole, and providing I kept selling cars nobody disturbed me.

My Friend Henry

The worst part of the previous seven days had been when the current girlfriend, Eileen, had told me she did not want to see me anymore.

It had not been too much of a shock as we had been growing apart for some time, also she was some years older than myself, a legal person in her own right and discarded boyfriend's as one would a sweet wrapper. Nevertheless, what I would miss, was her need for me and lying on her back with those beautiful legs, and what she could do with them when locked around me.

For some time before the miserable day she had told me the news of our separation, we had been invited to a birthday party over the following weekend. It was being held at a detached house in the country.

At the time I wanted to go but now I was not certain especially as I would be on my own. I had thought of phoning one of my old flames to see if she would join me, and when I did I was promptly told where I could get off, and it was not said very nicely.

This particular invite was more dignified than some we had been asked to, where if you went without a companion then you were not welcomed. It also followed that the person who accompanied you, it was quite

My Friend Henry

possible they did not leave with you, as sometimes during the event a game of changing partners would prevail..

With nothing else to do and knowing there would be friends there to commiserate with and perhaps some friendly lady to give me some sympathy. I got dressed in the fashion of the moment and made the journey.

On arrival at the large period property surrounded by trees, I knew I had made the right decision as I immediately cheered up when the drinks started to flow along with the jokes and chit chat. Although during the evening the memory of a white skirt kept appearing in my mind.

That was because as I drove up to the house, I had found an empty parking space to leave the car in front of the property. As I was locking it, I watched Mike, arm in arm with a girl in white and another couple going inside through the front door.

I had known him for a long time. Once, some time ago, we had been very close but no longer as we had gone our different ways. As was usual on the far side from where I was standing he had a lovely looking woman on his arm.

My Friend Henry

I just got sight of a fashionable white full skirt as it swirled out around her as they vanished inside.

It was a great party and there were a lot of people in the house to celebrate the host Nigel's, fiftieth birthday. He is an Insurance Broker, clever, tall and always smartly dressed and a very charismatic man and it seemed as if he had invited all of his clients to the event. My invitation came because of my ability to sell motor insurance to my car buyers.

Once there I found plenty of company in old friends most in a similar business to myself. The drinks were varied and plenty, everyone with a glass in their hand as we stood in a group near the large bay window chatting and exchanging stories. I had half expected Eileen to turn up with some new fellow on her arm, but the evening was to pass and she did not materialise.

I was surprised to see Rob, who was a very dear old friend on his own, as normally his future wife Wendy, was by his side., They were getting married the following March, five months away and I was to be their best man. Then gazing around I saw her, looking as elegant as ever sitting with some other ladies around a table in another part of the room.

My Friend Henry

One of the group was telling a story and at the end we all laughed...giggled would be more appropriate, as we had all heard it before. After which I excused myself and went over and invited Wendy to smooch with me around the floor, I say smooch as there was not much room for dancing on the tiny space available. We were like brother and sister together and felt natural in each other's company and spoke freely and easily about a number of things while she commiserated with me over the breakup with Eileen.

After a few pleasant turns around the floor talking about the wedding and some other silly things, I returned to the company. I was feeling very relaxed and was enjoying the chit chat, and then I'm not sure what made me turn but I had a feeling of being looked at.

When I did the rest of the room seemed to disappear into a misty babble. In sharp focus was an attractive pair of eyes adorned in a lovely face above a white skirt and looking at me. Our eyes locked together. Lovely feelings were cursing through me. She broke away and turned slightly as if she had had the same thoughts as myself. And then briefly looked back and smiled wiggling her hips. Then she turned her back and the moment was gone although burned on my brain.

My Friend Henry

I was in a quandary as I twisted round back to the group and tried to catch up with the conversation, although my mind would not or could not grasp it. One thing I was sure of before the evening was over, I would find out more about the lovely lady in white.

Although I tried to attract her attention again it did not happen, and on the couple of times it did, she would smile and turn away. I felt it was a game of catch me if you can. As much as I wanted to, I decided not to go over and have a chat with Mike. Quite frankly I did not like the man and it would possibly only start an argument, as he could be very sarcastic, and that was not the impression I wanted the lady in white to have of me.

My pulse had not really slowed down from the encounter and I was still full of those lovely eyes and the accompanying 'come to me' smile. I was not really paying attention to the people I was with.

It was Rob who broke the thoughts racing through my mind. As I said Rob was an old school friend. In a lull in the conversation because the music had changed and had been replaced by a much-loved tune of the time.

My Friend Henry

As it came blaring out of the music centre, it transformed the atmosphere as the people were singing or humming to it. He came close to me so I could hear him above the noise, holding me gently by the arm he spoke into my ear. "I know she is lovely and she is lovely...but don't get involved, she will only tease you."

I looked at him in surprise as I had not realised, I had been that distant from the group, and my feelings were on show. I faced him with a questionable look also feeling a little stupid. He smiled and looking in the direction of the group on the other side of the room saying "Sally...the lady in white!"

I was devastated and yet I did not know why. I did not know her...or had not even spoken to her, just the strong cosy memory of that brief exchange. The look in her beautiful eyes giving an indication of wanting to get to know me.

In my mind it was just a short encounter across a crowded room of two souls wanting to be together. A few seconds of the heart beating faster...the thought was difficult to remove from my head. I nodded in response.

My Friend Henry

Turning to him and trying to change the subject, if only to try and remove the image. I spoke in a stuttering voice of the football team we followed and how they would get on at the next match.

"The look on your face tells me you are not thinking about soccer...if it helps she works at Roneo's, I think in reception." Remember Rob was an old school friend and knew as much about my sexual needs, probably more than me. As he had been one of the four who had been in a kind of initiation ceremony. But more about that later.

I smiled and looked at him quizzically "Why is it you know all this about her and I have never seen her before?"

He looked over at her back, before saying "As you say I don't remember her coming to one of our parties or get togethers...but my sister works with her and I met her at one of their staff do's." I looked at him and had a feeling he was not telling me everything, so I said "And?"

"And nothing!" He looked away from me at the group across the room. "Let us just say we did not get on very

My Friend Henry

well...anyway it was a long time ago well before I met Wendy" He turned away and picked up his drink.

I didn't like talking about sex as I found it embarrassing but I couldn't resist saying "So she wouldn't let you get your leg over?"

He took a sip of his drink as if he was considering how to answer. "Something like that! The problem is...or was!" He shrugged his shoulders again before continuing "She is a nice lady and great company, but very sad in some ways and I think it is because it is difficult to be alone with her as her father insists on collecting her, and..."

He then shrugged his shoulders again as if what he was going to say did not matter. Although for the rest of the evening I tried to catch her attention, occasionally she would respond with a quick smile before turning away.

Suddenly, an elderly man came in and Sally was getting up to leave. The others in the group including Mike still had a drink in his hand and just ignored her. Sally collected her handbag, she twisted and seeking me out smiled and did a little dance and gave a little wave before turning and was walked out of the door.

My Friend Henry

Then the lovely lady in white was gone. Rob said "That was Daddy he has come to collect her, you have now seen first hand what I mean"

For me the room seemed suddenly empty. I looked at him "Is it always like that? He just nodded, and said "He is an executive with a Japanese Company and worries about morality and his daughter getting into trouble..."

Chapter Three

The Ride Continues

The earlier versions of this car had a bench type seat, easier to slide across and be close to your companion. Now, like all other models, bench seats had been discontinued and I guess for safety reasons  because if a driver went around a corner a bit sharpish, he could slide away from the steering wheel. Dangerous!

This edition of the car was different and more comfortable for driving, as the chair like arrangement held you firm. The gear lever and hand brake were on the floor between the individual passenger spaces, so moving onto the other seat was not very easy.

The temptation was strong, especially from Henry, to take her in my arms. However, if the answer was anything like the previously then I would be feeling foolish and making myself irritated.

My Friend Henry

We were totally relaxed and singing along to the music also laughing at silly things. Earlier Sally had released the buttons of her blouse showing the soft white of the top of her breasts. She was playing with the hem of her skirt keeping in time to the beat of the song.

A sign appeared on the side of the road indicating there was a 'lay-by' in another half a mile. I took hold of her hand and trying to sound casual as I was trembling at the thought of holding her, I said "Shall we stop for a while?"

She didn't answer at first and carried on singing, she seemed to be thinking about it. She looked over at me with that beautiful smile and just shook her head before saying very softly "No, let's carry on it is getting late." And then continued on singing and enjoying the melody and the harmony coming from the car's speakers.

I thought to myself as the rest area slipped past, 'Perhaps it was not such a good idea to stop and be restricted to the confines of the car, it would have been fun but in about another hour we should be at our destination and then the joy of being together in total privacy. I could see her in my mind's eye getting ready and waiting for me.

My Friend Henry

Sally's mind was racing at the thought of lying with a man for the first time. Her mother's voice screaming at her 'Do be careful, that is why you have a brother I did not want because I let a man get too close.'

At the time she had found the remark strange and it was something she frequently thought about. Her brother was ten years younger than her, with red hair whilst her own was blond. Her father's was dark and yet the landlord of the local public house was bright red. Her mother used to work there...did she let him get too close? It also followed was she a mistake? There was certainly not much of a loving relationship in the family.

She remembered quite clearly the first time a man tried to make love to her. Love was not the right word, having her was better. Sixteen years old and it had been her first job interview. She had been very nervous on entering the office for the consultation with the Employment Officer to work in the Organisation. He was in his late twenties, she had guessed and smelling of 'Old Spice.'

My Friend Henry

At first the conversation between them was business like, and then it changed as he wanted to know if she had a boy friend?

She had thought it was a funny question and had shaken her head. He had got up and walked casually around the desk. She thought he was leading her to the door and then he had started to touch her which she found offensive.

She had gone cold and froze. He pushed her urgently against the wall. Trying to kiss her but she turned her head. Her mother's words came to her.' Suddenly he was lifting her skirt. She screamed and tried to slap his face and with an effort managed to push him away. Opening the door, she had fled.

The feeling of being needed that afternoon all that time ago, had dominated her. She had been surprised when her body started to react to him, and she knew at the time if she didn't put a stop to it he would have his way.

Sally remembered the strange feelings flooding through her. A wanting she had not experienced before. Since then she had managed to bury those desires but now they were at the forefront in her mind.

Chapter Four

My Early Years

The enjoyment of a loving partner and being together to enjoy the creation of a new life is everyone's delight and a basic need, well at least I think so.

Although I had similar pleasures in later life they were very much secondary, than wanting to be with a person in a loving relationship, which is far more important and probably as a result of my upbringing, which was very puritan.

My mother and father did not talk about the carnal side of living, and my sister and I were kept apart, and were not allowed to mix.

This was just after the Second World War when people had been deprived of most luxuries and manufacturers of lingerie were keen to make up for lost revenue during the period of restriction throughout the conflict by advertising their wares.

So, the only real time I saw a woman semi naked was when travelling on buses or in the tube stations, and then it would only be pictures of scantily dressed models.

My Friend Henry

Whilst on a journey at that time, there were a great many advertisements with fashion girls all partially dressed in underwear showing off the wares of the supplier. Nothing naughty or provocative.

My embarrassment at those pictures was complete and I would have to look away knowing I had gone red at the displayed flesh. As I had no knowledge of the female form these adverts left me in a state of wonderment, for as I got used to seeing them I would experience strange feelings making me even more embarrassed.

Sadly, a lot later after these events the pictures were banned by a religious Mayor of London.

In the road and around the area where I was brought up, there were not any children especially in the neighbouring houses, most of the folk were in the later part of life. So not only was my upbringing very strict it was mostly devoid of love. In my younger years I had no idea about sex or what the difference was between boys and girls.

The junior school I attended was a boy's only establishment, the girls' part was in a different building

My Friend Henry

with an adjoining playground, which we boys were not allowed to go near.

Some of the lads, who were in the senior part of the school and in their final term would shout or whistle at the young ladies as they passed. They would get severely reprimanded by the teachers for doing so.

I just smiled and was left wondering what it was all about. So on the whole us lads were convinced that the female was nothing to do with us and were not approachable.

One evening when I was about seven or eight, I was sitting in a chair, and although I was not permitted to converse or play games with my sister she was allowed to instruct me in the basics of education. She was four years older than me and her school marks were excellent.

I was repeating some words, parrot fashion, which she was teaching me. A sharp strong feeling started and I felt my penis was getting hot. I could feel it getting larger. Although I have just used the correct term in those days it was referred to as Willie, I did not know what it's real name was or any variations. It had not

My Friend Henry

occurred before and I did not know why it was becoming so different. It was very frightening.

The ache in me was enormous...nothing sexual or any desire with it. I could not understand what was happening. It seemed ready to burst and I was almost in tears when I called my mother. She came in the room quickly and I was too embarrassed to say what was happening and just pointed in the direction of the arousal.

It did not take her long to understand the problem. Without inspecting the difficulty, she walked out and called my father. He came into the room and without looking, turned around to mother saying, 'There is nothing wrong, it's just that he's becoming a man.'

The whole event left me traumatised. Within a short time and much to my relief, it returned to its normal size. In the meantime my sister had been banished from the room and no more was said. And I was left wondering what he meant by 'me becoming a man?'

Chapter Five

Holiday Cottage

After the suggestion of pulling into the lay-by, we looked at each other and laughed and continued on our way. I changed the tape in the control unit and a complete set of new  songs filled the air in the car and light-heartedly we continued the journey .

The car surged on and according to the clock on the dashboard there was still another hour or so until we would reach our destination, a small holiday cottage near to the sea.

At one part of the music, which Sally was singing along to, she did a little dance with her feet on the floorboards of the car, smiling at me those eyes shining as she continued the song. She lifted the hem of her skirt and flicked it back and forth calypso style. I was so very happy as she looked so sweet, also as she was in high spirits was wonderful company. Henry thought so too.

My Friend Henry

Sally was laughing and singing along to the music, but above all alive with excitement and the anticipation of arriving at the cottage. She had strange feelings, unusual feelings. Her breasts felt different, more alive. Earlier Sally had felt the need to open her blouse and sensed the excitement flow through her when she saw the look on his face. She was a little sad deep inside when the lay-by slipped past...it would have been so easy to have stopped and held him. Nonetheless, she knew in her heart it was better to wait and be lost in the comfort and the privacy of the cottage.

She could not help contemplating what would it be like when he finally laid with her...would he be kind and gentle? The thought of when it would happen sent exciting messages in her. But above all would she enjoy being different or would she feel revolted?

Chapter Six

The Innocent Years

Let's look at history for a moment! In the years following the Second World War and into the nineteen fifties, people were starting to shake off the strict moral code of the Victorian period of the eighteen hundreds, which had been an era of narrow mindedness about the delights of the body, and had continued into the early nineteen twenties.

In some ways they were still being mimicked but in a less strict way as most parents and the elderly had been taught as children the harsh moral codes of the time.

Women did not dress provocatively their skirts were always below the knee and they rarely wore trousers, they were called slacks at the time, as the 'trousers' would have connotations of cross dressing, something which did not happen, at least not in public.

That is not to say in the main girls were very careful about their looks and took pride in their appearance. It meant nothing as far as I was concerned, and in a sad sort of way I got on with life not really understanding what it was all about.

My Friend Henry

My description above in the previous chapter of the upbringing was not too different to others ... except perhaps the lack of the teaching of the sexual act. As that was the responsibility of the parents, not the education in school. But it never occurred in our home.

I progressed through my early schooling with good marks. Although I made friends during teacher's time, they lived too far away to be able to continue with the relationship after school time came to an end in the late afternoon. As I left junior school it was very different when I moved to the upper discipline where I discovered and made new friends and associates.

A group of them, including Rob, who I mentioned earlier, lived not too far from me, just a short walking distance to another turning. I should add as a young boy I was not allowed to go that far away from home, that is why I did not get to know them socially when I was in the junior school.

We always congregated round one of the houses and normally it was that of the elder of the group, John. It was a large property rented from the Council boasting a very large garden on a corner plot.

My Friend Henry

Innocent times! We turned the ground to the rear of the house into a wonderland. There were small roads laid out round the perimeter for the dinky cars to travel on...in what sort of game I cannot remember.

There was so much to do, and it only took imagination to develop some genius form of activity. All great, naive, chaste like games, the adult world was of no concern to us.

One severe winter when the snow had covered the ground to six or more inches deep, we made blocks out of it. Mimicking the Eskimos and built an igloo in the similar rounded shape with a small entrance as we had seen in pictures. We did not get to use it as cats got in and the smell was not to our liking.

But the main home of the group was in the garden where the steel air raid shelter had been. This had been removed after the War leaving a large hole. Before my arrival, and some time before I joined them, they had built a den, large enough for the group to sit in.

It was nothing grand and made up of pieces of wood and some tin sheets. Nevertheless, it was private to us and a place to be out of the weather when it turned unpleasant.

My Friend Henry

Without being boring...well I hope so, before going any further it is important for the story so that the reader can identify and have empathy with this time in our history.

John, our accepted leader, would be fourteen that year the school leaving age, and he would be going out in the World to find work as an adult. Very different from today where boys of that age are still treated as children.

This was a time when there were no pictures in the newspapers of semi naked or naked women. Reporting was more serious. There were of course adverts in the female form.

The news on the BBC was broadcast twice or maybe three times in twenty four hours. There were very few female newsreaders on television, which in itself was only broadcast a few minutes a day. The ladies that did appear always wore high necked blouses, maybe dresses, but who knew as you were not allowed to see lower than the neckline. And sex was never spoken of. Young women when they went out in the evening would be chaperoned and normally father would be waiting at the bus stop to escort them home.

My Friend Henry

We are talking of a time when boys were growing into young men with the need for relief from their sexual urges and the demands of the monster in their trousers. I had stopped wondering why it got firm and accepted it and waited for it to return to normal.

In an average family environment there would be the sexual innuendoes when sisters or brothers got married and the nudge...nudge about activities in the bedroom. So, children would know or have an inkling about adult conduct. I knew nothing of this as most of the time I had been alone.

Chapter Seven

A Brutal Lesson

It was a wet afternoon and we had stopped a game we had been playing and retired to the den before getting too wet. We were sitting as normal on these occasions in a circle, and it turned out to be a day when I was to learn about life, and the memory would stay with me.

John had been telling stories of his sister who slept in the adjoining bedroom to his. The others had got excited when he explained the thumping and the noise her and her new husband had made on their wedding night.

It is half term and the school was closed, which meant all the adults were at work. I saw one of the others holding himself as John continued to explain the noise and for effect demonstrated by moving his groin in and out.

One of the group said it has been sometime since we had gone up stairs. The others started making comments which I did not fully understand. I sat listening to the remarks trying to recognize what they were referring to. John said, "I think the new-be should play the girls part."

My Friend Henry

I suddenly had a funny feeling as the others were looking at me as if they wanted to devour me. I did not know what to say. Then I thought maybe we were going to act a play or something.

Then Rob who was sitting next to me said "Are you up to it?" I did not realise it then but things were going to be anything but innocent.

They had all gone serious and were waiting for my answer. I tried to smile but I think it came out more as a frown as I shrugged my shoulders and said in a small voice "I suppose so!"

Then I looked around them and I was aware they were looking excited and intense. "What am I supposed to do?" I asked. They all looked at each other again before John said "We fuck you" I had never heard the word before so I had no idea what it meant. And then he continued "Nobody will be home for a long while so we will go, as normal into my bedroom in the house."

Trepidation was sweeping through me, I did not know what to expect. The group seemed so aggressive something I had not sensed before.

My Friend Henry

As soon as we were in his room John started taking his shirt off and the others were quick to follow. Thoughts were sweeping through me 'What sort of game was this if they needed to undress?'

Our leader was undoing the buttons on his trousers the others were following. They looked at me standing looking and feeling stupid. John said in a sharp voice "Come on Dennis, get your clothes off."

I reluctantly started to undo the fastenings on my clothing. The revulsion and horror was increasing in me as I watched them removing their day things and then their undergarments. They stood in a ring with their slim bodies glistening in the light from the window; their man hood growing in arousal.

They demanded I take the rest of my things off including my pants. I had never before been in a situation of standing in front of people with no clothes on. Even at home that did not happen.

It had gone too far now for me to back out, so I put a brave face on it and did what they wanted and lowered my shorts.

My Friend Henry

By now I was wondering what they had planned. Surely it couldn't be that bad. I had this strange pleasurable feeling as I stood in front of them in my socks, otherwise totally naked.

Unlike theirs, which were standing out strong and firm as they held them, mine was small and limp. I guess it was because of the shock of the event and the speculation of what was going to happen, as I knew I was going to be the one to play some important part...but what? One of the group said "Hey, it reminds me of Henry!"

Henry was an elderly teacher in school who walked in a stoop and always looked frail and limp. However they were to learn later in the afternoon that Henry, this new name, he was not always like that.

They all had a little giggle at the remark but now they wanted to get down to the serious business and took my arms and led me to the bed.

We are talking about a time when all women had only had the vote in elections for twenty years and in general, they were very much subservient to men.

My Friend Henry

In the cinema couples did not get into clinches...yes, they cuddled but if they got as far as the bedroom then they stayed dressed. Certainly, with most of their clothes on without the hint of flesh, if they got on the bed, then the man had to keep both his feet on the floor. They would just talk about the story line of the film and not about sex.

Advertising pictures, with the exception of those on the underground, showed women in the kitchen nicely dressed preparing the food or perhaps cleaning, and the man went out to work and came home to be fed and looked after.

Women, were not supposed to enjoy the sexual act, and when pregnant they tried to hide it by lace up bodices across their stomach or balloon type dresses. If they were not married they went away for two or three months to have the child and then it would be put out for adoption. Children were told that babies arrived from heaven on a stork.

It was not until the middle of the sixties when sex was first in print and appeared in a book. 'Lady Chatterley's Lover' it was published by Penguin Publishers and certain pages halfway through became grubby where people had re-read the saucy parts again and again.

My Friend Henry

It portrays in detail where the groundsman undresses the Lady and the description is how he penetrates her while they are in the garden shed. The book was on everyone's lips when the publisher was taken to court for the obscene content.

The first time I believe that sex was shown on the cinema screen, was in 'The God Father' again in the late sixties. Even then nothing was shown only the indication of the lady pinned against a door and having her clothes lifted by one of the characters. The shot then went to the other side and showed the door panelling going in and out with an appropriate noise.

I was just about thirteen at this time with no knowledge whatsoever of the sex act. Very strange situation when comparing it with today's total knowledge by young and old.

So how was I to know what the others had planned? I thought I was going to have my bottom slapped in some ceremonial event. I heard them agreeing who was going to go first and not knowing what they were talking about, I thought it was strange but it meant very little.

My Friend Henry

It was a frightening way to learn about the facts of life. It was so brutal in that, in a few hours I went from being totally innocent about the actions of the creation of a new life, to a violent understanding of it.

At first I was in shock. When Henry was pleasured some time later then the understanding came to me with different thoughts.

The rest of the afternoon went in a blur, as they took turns. Although a little shamefaced I also felt happier after the event, for I now knew why Henry got hard and when played with what pleasures it gave and what it could achieve.

I also looked at women, especially girls differently and also understood what my father was doing. I had gone into my parent's bedroom some time before this event, concerned because I had heard my mother groaning. Both of them were fully clothed with him on top, her legs in the air and he was pumping away. Even after I had rapidly left the scene and although my parents were aware that I had seen them, neither of them explained what they were doing. At the time the event had left me puzzled and annoyed at my father, because I was certain he was hurting my mother.

Chapter Eight

Ola Van Horton, was only eight years old when her mother Lucy moved from the Netherlands' to London because of a decision made by the giant company she worked for.

At first Ola had found the new existence strange and so different from the friendships and way of life she had experienced before the move.

It was sometime before arriving in their new home her parents had divorced and the loss of their joint love she had found hard to accept.

However, the parting had been of some relief as her mother and father were constantly arguing, mainly over money, and sometimes silly little things. Both worked together in the Executive Wing for the same large Oil Company whose Head Office was in Amsterdam.

Her father had wanted his only child to live with him, but finally after a string of Court Cases her mother was given custody of Ola.

After the breakup it had become more and more difficult for the pair to work together in the same building so a decision was

My Friend Henry

made in that her mother would transfer to the Company's London Offices.

A home was found for the new arrivals whilst comfortable it was not ideal, nevertheless the pair settled into it. Ola had little knowledge of the English language as her first tongue was Dutch, which her family had always used at home.

Schooling was difficult because understanding the meaning of what was being said, meant she was frequently teased by her peers driving her into deep depressions. However she tried harder to comprehend the phrases and words which she did not recognize and eventually overcame the difficulty.

Her mother's income was substantial, so money was not a problem and after some months of searching they found a detached house to the North of the capital and settled down to a new life. Although Ola was aware of the conflict between her parents continuing, it had little effect on her.
As a teenager life was good for Ola, her school reports were always excellent, and the group of friends she had known since moving to the new locality were fun to be with.

There was a sharing of excitement amongst the girls as the summer ball of nineteen fifty five was approaching, and serious discussion of what to wear.

A new mood of fashion was developing amongst the young women, one of shorter dresses. However, for the special evening Ola had settled for a long shade of light green creation bought by both her parents.

My Friend Henry

It would be the last event with her friends at the school that they would attend, as they would be parting and moving on with their lives.

After a long break for the summer recess it was time to think of the future and the option of choosing further education and where that would take place.

Ola, encouraged by her mother, and supported by her father who was now a Director of the Oil Firm, arranged for the Organization to support her through University, this was with the intention when on leaving, and providing her marks were of a high standard, there would be a position of employment with them.

However, after four years of hard work and studying it did not quite work out that way. Whilst Ola's marks were excellent, and her future was secure sometimes Mother Nature has other plans as during this period the tall smartly dressed lecturers' image frequently got in the way of her thoughts.

On the sports ground adjacent to Bath University overlooking the old City with its marvelous buildings, a large marquee had been erected. Once more Ola was with fellow students who were there for their graduation and to celebrate the end of a learning period.

She was again wearing a long green gown showing off her youthful slim body and not too dissimilar to the one she wore at the School's Summer Ball all that time before.

My Friend Henry

Her father had flown over from Holland for the occasion, and by now he and her mother had run out of harsh words to say to each other and engaged in normal conversation, if only a bit stinted, all the same they both wanted the best for their daughter.

The tables were laid out with white cloths and people were mingling around chatting. A group of musicians were playing on a raised area adding to the atmosphere with soft music.

Ola had excused herself from her parents and was talking to a group of students whom she had spent most of her leisure time with, between studying. Jackie her closest friend nudged her shoulder "Your heartthrob is standing at the bar."

She looked in the direction indicated and dressed differently than most of the men, in smart casual clothing and a tweed jacket was Professor Palmer, who whilst not on the staff of the University, lectured there from time to time.

Ola blushed at the sight of him, although a lot older than her she had in the past made it known that she fancied him. She smiled at her friend and dragged her eyes away, trying not to look at him.

As the afternoon's events progressed and moved on with the presentation of the certificates to the group who were leaving. When it was her turn Ola was flushed with pride as she received her awards and could not help doing a little dance as she returned to the table.

My Friend Henry

The wine flowed freely during the delicious meal. Afterwards the group sat around chatting and listening to the music, whilst others were dancing. Even her parents were holding each other as they slowly moved around the floor.

Ola, had been watching the man of her dreams feeling all kinds of nice feelings flowing through her. After a while she stood up from the table and swaying to the music, although the drink was helping to achieve that, she went across the room and took the Professor by the arm and dragged him on to the dance floor.

Chapter Nine

Adulthood

The group of friends worked and played well together the unlawful sex was an occasional thing although fun not very important to our young lives. Playing games like football and cricket were far more important. We also liked riding our cycles sometimes departing on long rides or going through the woods and frequently chasing each other.

School days slipped past and John was the first to leave after which the group saw less of each other. The last year at school for me was not so exciting in the evenings, as each day I was encouraged by my parents to study hard for the final exam. I was hoping for good marks, which I finally achieved.

That is not to say it was totally boring. Vivian a lovely looking girl about the same age as me and lived a few doors down from our house and although we went to the same school, however the girls were in one part at going home time we lads had to wait while the females left, so there was no chance of mixing.

It was a bright sunny day with white clouds scudding across the sky and I was making my way home, As I was

My Friend Henry

passing a sweet shop Vivian walked out of it. When she saw me she went all coy and I am certain she blushed. We both stopped and looked at each other, I had a big grin on my face. I had been thinking and dreaming for some time of needing a conquest ... was she going to be it?

We walked home together after that meeting and she lowered her head and shyly said goodbye as we reached her gate and she quickly walked up the path. I strolled on. We both stopped as if by some internal signal and looked back at each other, she smiled and disappeared down the side of the house.

We were frequently seen walking home together and I think if either of us had been asked if we had some sort of arrangement we would have shook our heads. It was a tacit arrangement but somehow we managed to be together and the joy in my heart was total I so dearly wanted more to happen.

It did develop into seeing each other at weekends and sometimes with a group of acquaintances and she became recognised as my girl friend. All the while I wanted more. There was no agreement with my clumsy innuendoes and any time I tried to explore the inner workings of the dresses she wore, the answer was

My Friend Henry

always a gentle no, or silence and my hand being pushed away.

It was one rainy day and it was lashing down and what turned out to be a group walk in the woods was cancelled because of the inclement weather, it was decided an afternoon at the cinema was a great idea. The group entered the sparkling foyer of the picture house and by some silent agreement vanished in pairs into the vast space.

Vivian and I made ourselves comfortable in two seats in the back row for the afternoon film show. After some touching and kisses Henry was delighted when he got his fair share of excitement as he was handled lovingly and to his mind very satisfying as fingers found his smoothness ... me I got no further than the top of a silk covered knee.

After that momentous occasion we saw each other frequently normally at weekends and sometimes, when the situation allowed, we explored the differences in each other and I became very familiar with the shape of a stocking covered knee while Henry didn't find a 'Holiday home' but nevertheless finished with some form of gratification.

My Friend Henry

Going out to work was a large shock to the system because suddenly instead of the brief school days with the times of rest, I was subject to an early start and a ten hour day, and sometimes longer before getting home again.

Nobody, my parents or the teachers at school, had prepared any of us prior to the occasion of going out to work and the sudden change in life style. Ah, but there were exciting times in between.

I was training in the exhilarating world of electrics … okay … a dog's body for an electrician. We were on call to remedy problems when the power had ceased to exist at a home or sometimes plush offices.

It was one of these places that I met Eileen, a happy go lucky young woman older than me, training to be a solicitor. At first, I thought nothing of it until one day I was crawling under the back of a desk to fit some electrics to a wall.

Suddenly there was some shuffling going on beside me and looking up I saw the most beautiful sight of a shapely pair of nylon clad legs disappearing up into a skirt. I was feeling uncomfortable although Henry had made a note of the sight and was twitching.

My Friend Henry

The silence dragged on and I with shaking hands managed to continue what I was doing. I was about to finish the work when a sweet tinkling voice said 'mind what you are doing down there and no looking.' I relaxed as she had broken the ice and I did not feel so embarrassed.

I was terrified for I had never been in this situation with a female and I did not know what to do or how to deal with the circumstance. I crawled out from behind the desk and a pair of eyes smiled at me making my heartbeat faster and Henry to my further embarrassment decided he wanted to be involved but was disappointed as he was not needed.

It was sometime later at the same solicitors Christmas party, which our firm had been invited to, Henry and I got on well with Eileen with me exploring the female form and Henry at last finding a 'Holiday home' which to his mind the stays were far too short. From an awkward start to our relationship it was sealed in a comfortable long lasting friendship even more so as the carnal part was sealed with no demands.

In that period after the War, young men at the age of eighteen were obliged to carry out National Service and serve time in the Forces for two years. This continued

My Friend Henry

until nineteen sixty three when the Government decided to end the requirement.

So, it was sad when I received my call up papers, for now life would be totally different and I would no longer have the opportunity of seeing the person who taught me many things about manhood.

It was Springtime and another untimely start with the early morning sun's rays pouring in through the bedroom window, giving me a wonderful lift and a great feeling as I prepared to leave and start a new and exciting life.

The Army had supplied me with a pass for travelling, which when I arrived at the railway station I presented to the ticket collector. He smiled for obviously he knew where I was going as he directed me to the first of a few trains to take me to the Army camp where I was to be assessed for my time in the Forces.

Looking back now, the travel arrangements the Army had arranged, were so old fashioned comparing it with today. It was a steam train with a locomotive blowing soot and smoke out of the funnel at the front of the machine, as it chugged into the cold draughty platform of the station.

My Friend Henry

It took most of the day to travel from London, changing onto different trains for the journey. The final one was in Cardiff where a very slow column of scruffy carriages took me to the administration camp, tucked in between the hills of Wales.

Although it was thrilling to be away from home for the first time on my own, it was a little depressing when my only personal private area was a bed in between a row of others. I missed the seclusion of my bedroom. The surroundings were in a long type of dormitory in what was no more than a wooden hut, cold or very hot depending on the outside weather.

The following day we, that is myself and the other new recruits, were called up at the crack of dawn for the day's activities. After a tasty breakfast, although the fried eggs I found were a little hard, we were marched off, with a soldier who had three stripes on his arm, in which I was later to learn was a Sergeant. He was shouting most of the time at what was an untidy line of new recruits, still in civvies, to get in step. We halted outside the medical centre where we formed a single line and entered the building.

An orderly, or perhaps he was a nurse, told us to remove our coats and roll up our sleeves. He then went down the

My Friend Henry

line administering, with the same needle, well I did not see him changing it, some form of injection in the upper part of the arm. The line moved forward and those at the head disappeared behind a canvas screen. I was wondering what went on behind it.

When it was my turn there was a medico who ran a stethoscope over my chest and then sitting on a chair in front of me, told me to drop my trousers. With some reluctance I did what he wanted.

I stood in front of him feeling a little nervous and a bit stupid when Henry was released from his comfort zone. He was still limp and waving in the fresh air. Which surprised me as the doctor was in no hurry and slid on rubber gloves, and lifted Henry up and was holding him, usually he liked this form of treatment   and would normally become very full of itself. All I wanted was to pull up my trousers and under garments.

Leaning forward the Doctor adjusted his glasses on the end of his nose and inspected my private parts as if they were something quite different. What surprised me Henry was still not interested. With one hand he had lifted him up and felt around him. The doctor seemed satisfied and made some notes on a form, then

My Friend Henry

he let my limp friend go. I was told to get dressed and I was allowed to leave.

I learned later he was checking to see if I had a rupture. I don't know if that was true or not. More likely it was to see if there was any venereal disease.

Chapter Ten

Sally *all her life she had been protected by her father to the point of domination. It had not got any better as she bloomed into adulthood. At first, she had seen her parents attitude as being loved and wanted, but as time went by she found it suffocating.*

In her last year in school she was jealous of her friends who had far more freedom, and would listen to their stories of going out on dates with a heavy heart and envy.

When she had first seen Dennis, he had followed them into the room shortly after their arrival at the party with the group she was with, her heart had flipped and she had a strong desire of wanting to get to know him. It was a wonderful warm feeling.

She had tried to catch his eye on a number of occasions, but he was always chatting, or at one time dancing, and for some reason she had felt jealous because he was with the other woman. She scolded herself for the odd feeling.

My Friend Henry

Eventually their eyes had met. She was not an expert at flirting, but she had tried to make it clear she would like to see him and was so very disappointed, when he did not follow up the obvious invitation she was sending him.

And then they finally met. It was at a wedding and Sally had known for some time that he was to be the best man and was looking forward to it, all the time wondering what he would be like when they finally spoke.

She had not been disappointed. But then the horror of her father arriving when they were finally getting to know each other. She so much wanted to be alone with him, but it was forbidden.

Sally was so frightened that she would lose him that finally she started to make plans. She knew for certain her parents would not let her go away with him so it was pointless asking. So, without them knowing she asked him to take her away for the weekend.

It had been easier than she had first thought. She arranged to go to work on that Friday morning and after leaving at her normal time she had waited for her mother and father to leave the house. She then returned and packed a case and took it to her place of employment where she had arranged for Dennis to collect her at the end of the day.

Chapter Eleven

Out of Bounds

After some heavy months of training, and as I had been assigned to a Royal Engineering Regiment, the activities were centred around field craft, although the Army did not let us forget how to polish boots and brass buttons. Also, wherever we went we marched up and down keeping in step, and no matter what the conditions were like in the field, wet or dry, our kit was inspected to make certain it was clean and sparkling.

Eight weeks passed and each individual was told where in the world he was to be posted, which had to happen and the new friendships we had started to enjoy were broken up.

I was lucky as I was posted to an island in the Mediterranean Sea. On arriving there, very excited as it was the first time I had been abroad, I was assigned to office work and the skill of learning signal disciplines. There was nothing too strenuous in the work and an almost nine to five existence.

During the tour of duty, we were allowed to go on leave. My sexual experiences up to this time was being hampered by the Army's strict regulations. I was

My Friend Henry

missing my relationships of kissing and cuddling at dances or parties and what could follow on after the music had stopped. I was enjoying my time in the forces but now at the age of eighteen going on nineteen, I was experiencing a need and at night would frequently dream of the event, if only to please Henry.

There were four of us who were granted leave for seven days, there was no way we were able to go home to the U.K., it was too far and too costly and the Army were not paying.

But why would we want to as we were in the sun and not too far away from fine beaches and a holiday resort on the coast, and we could use an Army vehicle to get there.

There were also houses with red lights outside where we were told ladies were available. On the other hand, it was made very clear we were to stay out of them because if caught in one by the Military Police we would be in serious trouble ... that warning was enough to make us more curious.

It was after we had been a few days on the coast, with plenty of food and drink ... especially the drink. I was getting more excited daily listening to the others

My Friend Henry

explaining about their girl friends and descriptive activity, which they had experienced before being called up to join the Army. While listening I would be thinking of Eileen and her special ways.

The tales encouraged me to find out what was behind those red lights. I was becoming more and more resolute to appease my friend Henry and his constant requirement in the warmth of the sun and the skimpy clad females sunning themselves the urge became very strong.

We had been there a few days when one of the others in the group disappeared for a few hours, I thought I would do the same. He had visited one of those houses with a red light outside and was full of the details while explaining the experience.

It encouraged me although I really did not need much of it to do the same and with determination to go beyond a red light and satisfy the demands being made by Henry.

They were non-descript buildings with blacked out windows in alley ways and side turnings, in my mind offering an invitation to where it would be possible to satisfy the burning desire in me.

My Friend Henry

As each day passed, they seemed more and more attractive. Finally one afternoon, leaving the others I plucked up the courage to ignore the teaching of the Army and learn about the inner workings of the houses in red.

It was in a side street the back of which looked over the beach. I looked both ways up and down the road before gingerly pushing the door open. Inside there was soft lighting and the hum of a fan turning slowly hanging from the ceiling.

Sitting behind a desk was an elderly woman, who stood up with a grin on her face as I entered. She was wearing a long sari type dress which was wrapped around her. I assumed it was a woman, but I had my doubts for as she shook my hand, which I expected to feel soft, it was the opposite and seemed a bit course. Then she handed me a slip of paper with a sum of money on it, I dug into my back pocket and paid her. I could feel Henry getting interested in the proceedings.

She pointed to a door, which was guarded by a man in some form of beige uniform, and I was told to go in there. The guard, a big man, eyed me up and down as I passed him. I nervously entered a large room with about ten girls sitting around on couches and arm chairs in various forms of skimpy garments, most showing off their legs and leaving little to the mind's eye.

They all stood up as I entered. I was feeling a little stupid and wondering what had enticed me to go in there. And then I remembered it was Henry's idea.

There was also another guard, a large man dressed in a suit taking in the proceedings and I thought 'he had a grand job with all those females around him.'

Suddenly I was very nervous and swallowed hard, but my friend was showing more interest. The girls at first were looking at each other before turning their gaze at me, their eyes moving up and down making me feel like a piece of meat, which I guess I was, kind of.

Laughing and smiling they arranged themselves into a line. I was told to choose one, by another woman who was sitting in a padded armchair. Some of them were well built and looked a bit fearsome; my mouth had gone dry and my heart was pumping hard, I had not thought I would have to choose the girl. I pointed to the petit thing with long black hair on the end of the line.

She was wearing a slinky, small light blue dress, signalling the picture of her breasts with twin nipples

My Friend Henry

pressing forward. It was low and off the shoulder with small straps for support, also it was short...very short far above the knee showing slim brown legs.

She sort of drifted over to me, on high heeled shoes and a big grin on her face, glancing back at the others as if to say 'he's mine', before she reached me.

I am wondering where we were supposed to carry out the action. For one horrible moment I thought it was going to be on one of the settees in front of everyone, but I had a feeling Henry would like that.

With a soft warm hand she took hold of mine and led me to one of the doors off to one side, which led into a small space not much larger than a closet. Still smiling she leaned against the door with her back and closed it.

The room was extremely shadowy with very little light coming in through a small window, more like a vent to my right. There was limited furniture except the bed, with on top what looked like a not very clean mattress.

I stopped totally frozen not knowing how to proceed. Do I just grab her? She stood in front of me with a grin on her face. The low luminosity from the partly blanked cut window highlighting her sun-tanned shape.

My Friend Henry

Without hesitating she leant slightly forward and took hold of the hem of the dress and instantly peeled it off over her head. Her totally naked body was on display close enough to touch.

Two small firm round breasts, with hard nipples mimicking the shape I had seen when they were covered in the blue material. My eyes were glued to them as I was reminded of such wonderful beauty.

As I looked over her perfect form I could feel Henry getting very hard. This solved the problem of me having embarrassing thoughts, because of the strange situation and anxiety in me of the important part - Henry, not reacting.

I had discovered a long time before that event that I had little control over Henry who had a mind of his own, and now he wanted to prove his worth.

I stood feeling a little stupid, trembling slightly. I could not take my eyes off her slim sun-tanned body, and especially her breasts; all the time feeling Henry growing strong and hard.

On a small table there was a bowl of steaming water which she put on the floor in front of me, at the same

My Friend Henry

time telling me her name was Patsy. She said it so casually, it was as if she was inviting me to a tea party. Stuttering, I murmured something in reply.

I had a feeling of numbness maybe because I was disobeying regulations causing a numbness and not knowing how to proceed as strange these feelings raced through me.

Did I just take hold of her and see what happened? There had been no need for me to worry as she sat on the bed in front of me and leaning forward expertly undid my shorts and pushed them down, followed by my under things.

She was taking her time fondling Henry reminding me of how strong and it felt as if my whole being was encased in this monster who stood to attention, for Henry knew he was going to be pleasured.

Unusual strong sensations were running through me as she washed Henry and then dried him with a towel. She was looking at me. She slowly held her arms open and invited me on top of her. I was too excited for the act to last very long and shortly after I was standing outside the back door looking out over the beach and the sea, feeling a new man.

Chapter Twelve

After the event at the leaving Prom, Ola was offered, as was promised, a position with the Oil Giant. Putting all thoughts of the Professor behind her she took to the vocation precisely and accurately. She enjoyed the work, it suited the way she thought and because of it, Ola looked forward to each day and was delighted to be given new challenges. She was frequently told by her immediate managers who were very pleased with her, that her future was bright.

All that changed when one day whilst walking down a carpeted corridor near the Executive suite, carrying some ledgers, she was shocked to see Professor Palmer. He had come out of a side room and she probably would not have seen him, but when he said "Can I help you with those?" she nearly dropped them, and she could have swooned when he took them out of her arms.

Before joining the Company she had had no idea it was the same organisation where the Professor was normally employed when he wasn't lecturing at the various University's.

My Friend Henry

His personal office was in the same building where Ola worked, although he was frequently away travelling to the various sites where they drilled for oil around the world, so before that day she had not been aware of his existence in the company.

Over the following weeks a school crush developed into something more profound. They frequently met during the lunch time period allowing their relationship to develop and become stronger. The big difference in their ages vanished and became meaningless to them.

It was not quite a year after the meeting in the corridor when her father flew over from Holland to walk her down the aisle when the pair were married. Although Ola carried on working the excitement of making a home became her priority.

Another year was to pass and very much to both parents disappointment she decided to leave the company. The pair had been trying for a child and it was not happening. Ola, with natural maternal instincts egging her on, was convinced it was the pressure of her employment, which was preventing the happening.

She was not to know until sometime later, that he had taken precautions against becoming a father long before they were married.

Chapter Thirteen

The Gate

The road was curving round to the right, a long comfortable turn for the car so there was no need to reduce speed. Out of sight and further round the bend I saw the glimmer of headlights coming towards us but I  did not see them as a problem.

Sally asked if I could put the heating on as her feet were cold. I nodded my head and briefly took my eyes off the road. I was very aware of the controls on the previous model of the car however, in this version they had been changed.

As I could not do it by touch alone I looked down to find the small silver lever, which was in a slide, and to adjust the warmth I needed to move it to one side.

A piercing scream and white light flooding the interior of the car, made my heart go into overdrive. I looked back at the road and coming straight towards us was

My Friend Henry

that other car I had seen in the distance. My guess the driver was taking the bend too fast and had lost control and was on our side of the road.

To our left there was a wide gravelled area with a dark high surround. I could not quite see in the limited light as the headlights were facing the way the car was travelling and that was not where I wanted to go to avoid a head on collition. There was no time to consider the implications of turning on to a soft surface at the speed we were doing.

I turned the steering wheel knowing if I touched the brakes the car would slide and I would lose control. The other car was starting to turn away from us, but it was very close.

Our car responded well, it slid a little, which I was able to manage. The lights swung round and illuminated the new direction. We were surrounded by high hedges with what I thought at first, and there were no breaks in it.

Then I saw the five bar gate which was closed. It was directly in front but slightly to one side of us and was the closed entrance to a field. The other car hurtled past missing us but far too close to feel comfortable about it.

My Friend Henry

Quick calculations were going through my head. I could not see how I was going to be able to change direction and get back on the road, without losing control when the tyres lost their grip on the loose surface of gravel.

The small opening between the solid gate posts was not much wider than the car. The car was going straight for the left hand support which was wide and of a solid stone construction. I did not dare to brake in case we slid straight into the solid gate post.

There was no choice, although it was shut, the gate was the only answer. We swept towards it. It looked large as it was flooded by the headlights.

I adjusted the steering to miss either of the posts and hit the gate in its centre. Pieces of wood illuminated by our lights cascaded in the air and over the car as we went through the small gap destroying the structure but missing the danger of the supports.

We were thrown forward with the impact. We were bumping across a grassy field. There did not seem to be any damage to the beautiful car from Longbridge as the headlights were still working and still aligned as before.

My Friend Henry

Slowing our pace as the car was sliding on the wet grass. I gently steered it in a circle and came back out through the broken gate with parts still attached to the hinges. Taking great care as we drove over the gravel on leaving the field and then I turned on to the road.

As all this was happening another car went past, I didn't give it any thought as I was still getting over the event of the near miss of a head on collision and going through the closed gate.

I stopped on the side of the road to inspect for any damage; it was remarkable there was very little, a piece of wood stuck in the grill which I removed.

Satisfied it was safe to continue I re-joined Sally. She turned and leaned over towards me and put her arms around my neck and was visibly shaking as she held me tight.

After a while she kissed me on the lips. It was beautiful. My heart was pounding for a different reason. She looked into my eyes smiling before moving back to her seat. The whole event was worth it just for that wonderful moment. Shortly after I put the car in gear, and we were back on the road resuming the journey.

Chapter Fourteen

Smitten

The following day after the party where I had first seen Sally, I was in a quandary. Those beautiful eyes were in my mind. I could not get the feeling out of my head of looking at her, and the tug of some form of magic between us. A number of times I picked up the telephone to ring her and held it in my hand trembling but did nothing.

I had previously looked up the number of where she worked and noted it down on a pad on the desk in front of me. Each time, after lifting, and holding the receiver while staring into space but not making a decision, I put the phone down. After all she was with that thing called Mike and I was certain he would claim her as his. Knowing him he would have forced himself on her and as usual would broadcast it around town.

After a few days the desire was getting less, although the feeling of wanting to see her did not completely go away. I finally managed to put the thought of her behind me and got on with my life and work.

The reaction of seeing her for that brief moment which had flooded through me never went away and little things would trigger it, just seeing someone in a white dress or skirt would have feelings flooding through me.

The months drifted past and in the evening or the weekend I would go to my usual haunts. The darts team I belonged to also played at different venues, which was nice as it made a change. And on occasion I would meet someone from the past and a few times without any planning would be caressed or doing the caressing in a strange situation, which was good for my bruised ego and Henry's enjoyment.

Selling cars for a living can be very rewarding, but there is the downside, as one has a need to be vigilant and to react to a potential buyer when they show interest in a model.

The premises where I worked with a team of others, although covered with a substantial roof was open on three sides and when it was wet, raining and cold it was not very pleasant, as one needed to stand with the vehicles and look interested.

There were three of us that looked after the selling side of the large organisation. On a raised area with a balcony around it, overlooking the site, were the sales offices. One of which was for an elderly Sales Manager

My Friend Henry

who in the main dealt with trade enquiries and was helped by Julie, a nondescript young woman, always smartly dressed although not in the current fashion, while her face had a smile for everyone.

There was not a man amongst the team from the car cleaners to the mechanics who did not treat her with respect. That was because she had the ear of the management. In another building close by were the main offices of the company where the accounts were kept managed by a team of young men and women.

Although I had nearly forgotten about Sally, and as I said from time to time the thought of her would come flooding back especially if triggered by a small event. It was that sort of occasion when one evening playing darts and at the end of the bar a woman was standing with her back to me with long flowing blond hair and for a moment I thought it was Sally. Disappointment flooded through me when she turned and it was nothing like her.

I really needed to get her out of my mind but there was no one who I found attractive enough to want to be with. I thought of ringing my old flame Eileen, but then I could not summon up the enthusiasm to do it, and instead would find something to keep me busy.

My Friend Henry

It was a dreary type of day when a couple arrived on site. She looked in her late twenties whilst he was some years older. They started to walk around the cars and I instantly knew by their actions they were in the mood to buy one. Both were well dressed in long coats to keep out the cold.

I introduced myself and they responded by saying they were Professor and Mrs Palmer, we shook hands. I already knew who they were as pictures of them had recently been in the newspaper when he was promoted to the board of one of the giant oil companies. He was an engineer and as the article said, travelled the world as the expert in the operation of oil drilling rigs.

I politely asked what sort of car they were looking for. He glanced at his wife as if trying to make a point about a previous discussion and said he wanted something roomy and powerful.

I walked with them around the site explaining about the vehicles in the various types of models. She was very pretty, in fact beautiful and knew it, as she had a way of being very feminine, she would look with a teasing smile and would frequently try the seating in a car by gently sliding in showing far more leg than I thought was necessary. I had the feeling the presentation was for my benefit.

They had been there for about an hour, he was pleasant and easy to talk to whilst his wife would flash her eyes and climb into another car.

After some time when I had got to the stage of running out of words in describing vehicles, they decided on a top of the range a GT Ford Consul medium size and fast.

I was certain he was not happy about it as it was nothing like the car he had described he wanted. Without a doubt the lady always got her own way in the relationship. I could not help noticing from time to time she would brush against me, and I am sure she made certain her husband did not notice.

We retired to the warm office, which was a relief to be out of the cold. They both took off their coats. I hung them on the coat rack. He was in smart casual clothes, jacket and tie. I realised for the first time he was a lot older than I first thought.

Mrs Palmer, now I had been introduced to her as Ola she had auburn hair flowing down to her shoulders. She was dressed to take any man's breath away ... a small tailored suit showing the swell of her breasts and with a very short skirt displaying her legs, which I had already seen most of. Henry stirred a little at the sight of her; I swallowed hard and showed them to chairs so we could complete the paper work.

I had a need to go into Julie's office to get the documents for the car they were buying as they were kept there under her control. She stood up and moved away from her desk to the filing cabinet saying "You had better be careful, she fancies you and you look smitten, would you like me to take over and do the final part of the sale."

I was astounded by her remark, she was not the type to talk about sexual matters. I felt hot as I did not realise my feelings were showing, I smiled and shook my head I did not want to miss being near the delectable Mrs Palmer and gently took the documents from her.

Back in my own office I started to go through the paperwork with them, which was a little difficult as my hands would not stop trembling, and my tongue was finding it difficult to form my words.

Those eyes with the long dark lashes frequently looked at me, which were turning my insides to jelly, and Henry was making a nuisance of himself. I explained the paper work describing how we would register the car in their name and when it was complete we would then deliver the documents to them. In the meantime they could take the car away today once they had paid for it.

It was a little time later, and it was with relief from the sexy woman when the transaction came to an end, and they owned the car and I was showing them the controls to drive it.

I watched as they drove away feeling a little stupid at the sensation, which had been with me since they had arrived. Mrs Palmer lowered the window to wave 'good bye' as the car swept out of the gate. For a brief time that afternoon my thoughts of Sally had vanished replaced by the charming beautiful Mrs Ola Palmer, but they quickly came back as I suddenly felt empty.

Chapter Fifteen

Entrapment

It was a few weeks later and a foggy misty type of day when the documents for their Ford Consul were returned to us by the registration authority.
I was sitting at my desk when Julie came in with a handful of paperwork for me to deal with, saying 'One of them in that pile is for your girlfriend.'

I did not know who or what she was talking about and I looked at her quizzically. She just smiled. I picked up the bundle and then, as I just said, the Palmer's document was amongst them. It did not take too long to see that they were in order as I quickly ran through them to make sure they were correct.

Normally one of the cleaners or the odd job man employed by the organisation would take them and deliver them to the client. However, on this occasion I could not get the thought out of my head of the beautiful Mrs Palmer, with the lovely legs and flashing smile. Henry twitched at the thought.

As I said, it was a cold and bitter day as I sat wrapped up in the warmth of the office, I thought it was too

My Friend Henry

frosty to be outside. Thinking the chances of anyone coming on the site to look at cars was very remote. Anyway, there were two other salesmen. So, I decided it would be better use of my time to deliver them myself.

After I explained to the manager my thoughts, he agreed with me and followed it by saying, 'It would be good for relationships as they were obviously affluent people, it would be far better from an image point of view for the original person dealing with the sale to deliver the documents.'

I must confess there was a feeling of excitement at the chance of seeing Mrs Palmer again. I telephoned to make arrangements to go there. A gentle low feminine voice, which I immediately recognised, answered the phone.

With my heart doing somersaults and Henry suddenly paying interest, my tongue stuck between my teeth as I tried to persuade it to work.

After explaining who I was in a faltering voice we arranged for me to go around later that very morning. I was feeling a little guilty by depriving one of the cleaners a trip out, but said to myself 'why shouldn't I take them, anyway the Manager had agreed?' With the

My Friend Henry

added thought 'of at least it would take me out of the cold for a short time.'

When I arrived it was nearly midday. It was a charming attractive detached property standing up a short drive, on which I parked the car. Well tended flower beds looking a little sad in the cold morning air, and gleaming paint work, were all around me. Feeling a little excited at the thought of that flashing smile, although I was certain in my mind of a feeling of being disappointed, as no doubt I would be dealing with the husband. I pressed the shining brass bell push; somewhere inside I could hear the muffled sound of the tuneful chimes.

As it turned out I was not disappointed, in fact overwhelmed when the white glossy door opened. It was not Mr Palmer. She smiled, with a red gown flowing around her.

Opening the entrance way further she stood to one side and told me to come in out of the cold. On entering the warmth of the hall she vanished into a room and left me standing with the file in my hand, I thought perhaps she had gone to fetch her husband.

My Friend Henry

She came back still wearing the satiny red house coat and smelling of expensive perfume, of which I was certain she had just adorned.

Taking the file from my hand and looking at it intensely, she raised her head and with a dazzling smile turned away from me saying "It will be more comfortable if we look at it in the lounge ... you had better come in case I need you to explain something."

The 'we' in her conversation gave me the impression of someone else not the meaning to be me. I thought to myself 'What could possibly need explaining it is a car registration document there is nothing in it to explain!' But then again, the longer I am near this beautiful lady the more I would like it. Without a doubt though I thought the Professor husband would be in charge of the conversation.

The room to the rear of the house was large bright and airy, with huge windows looking over a neat and well manicured garden stretching into the distance and being attended to by a gardener; I immediately knew it was not Mr Palmer he was too different and chunky where the other was slim. I thought 'he must be the person keeping the front looking pristine.'

My Friend Henry

She indicated to one of a pair of settees, which were in the middle of the room facing each other with the fire place glowing with imitation logs to one side in the centre, signifying for me to sit down.

Next to the unit was a drinks trolley with a variety of bottles and glasses on. With her hips swaying she looked over her shoulder and smiled at me as she glided over to the window in her red spiky high heels. Going to the corner of the room and using a cord pulled the thick heavy curtains together, they slid as one closing at the centre totally shutting out the view.

The room turned into an exciting softly lit sanctum and abruptly became exceptionally personal. I was getting hot and bothered as I was not certain at that stage what she had in mind. I was thinking it was getting out of hand and I should be getting back to the site. Trying to stay professional, however I could not stop Henry reacting.

She had put the paperwork down on a low unit. I was feeling uncomfortable. It felt wrong to be alone with another man's wife especially the way she was dressed. I said in a quiet stuttering voice "Don't you want to check the documents, as I need to get back to work?"

My Friend Henry

Those eyes burned into mine she was breathing slowly "Not really, I am sure they are fine, you are too much of an expert for them to be otherwise." And then added "I am sure you don't have to leave just yet."

The way she was scantily dressed with perfume and desire oozing from her. The thought of going back to the car site was fast disappearing from my mind, anyway Henry was wide awake and demanding the energy of what little was left of my determination to leave
She had moved gently and softly closer to me. As she moved the bright red of the shiny loosely tied house coat was showing a lot of nylon clad leg. My eyes followed every movement and taking in the splendour of her.

She leant over the drinks trolley. The garment fell forward giving me a view of most of a pair of smooth white breasts, with the hint of a red bra matching the colour of her hair. Holding a glass in one hand she picked up the whisky bottle and looking me in the eye said "I bet you could use one of these?"

I nodded my head as I had a feeling things were going to get very exciting, certainly Henry thought so.

My Friend Henry

She did a little swagger, swaying her hips again as she walked back from the trolley. The red house coat was switching open showing a matching suspender belt holding up dark coloured stockings covering her shapely legs.

She stopped and that beautiful smile swept over me, before leaning forward and again the house coat opened with a promise. She handed me the drink. My hand was trembling a little as she passed it to me.

She raised the glass in a form of salute before taking a sip from the one she had poured for herself. I could feel Henry paying a great deal of attention and the lump in my trousers was becoming prominent.

She sort of waltzed and glided back to the trolley where she replaced the bottle. With a smile in my direction she released the single tie on the house coat which finally fell fully open as she sashayed back and sat down closely next to me. I could feel the warmth of her, the perfume enveloping my being as if to capture me in her feminine charms.

The open red silky house coat was displaying more of Mrs Palmer. She was wearing it as a frame to her allure,

My Friend Henry

dressed skimpily in a small set of matching red bra and panties.

I did not move. It was her call. Henry had immediately jumped to attention and was demanding all the remaining vitality and was becoming very much in charge.

She reached over me and placed her unfinished drink on a side table next to me moving very close to me on the settee as she did so, I could feel the softness of her as our bodies touched. I still had not moved.

An arm stretched over me with glistening gold bracelets reflecting the light. Her hand slid down to my front and stroked the lump. All the time we were looking at each other, our eyes locked in their own game. My whole being had gone rigid and had disappeared into Henry.

I put the drink down next to hers, trying not to spill it as the tremor in my hand had increased. She slowly slipped around and was on her knees in front of me, looking up into my face her eyes flashing accompanying that big gentle smile.

Leaning forward over my knees I could see the beauty of her framed in the red of the robe, her nipples pressing sharply forward in her bra.

My Friend Henry

I felt dizzy with desire, deep emotions chasing through me. She moved nearer, one hand stroking the lump which was Henry, the other was looking for the zip fastening.

I was past caring, the anticipation and excitement flowing through me centring on Henry. The slim fingers adorned with gold rings, gently lowered the tag and the zip started opening. I almost screamed.

It was an exceptionally pleasant and unexpected few hours and I left there dragging myself away. Henry was in love and it was not easy to put him away as he was struggling to keep free. I wanted to see her again but the answer was no, she told me her husband, who worked on Oil Rigs and would be home in a few days, and I guessed it would be him who would be satisfying her sexual desires.

As I got to the door she was standing behind me, the tie on the coat was no longer attached. Her beautiful form now totally naked with the exception of the red high heeled shoes, was framed in the folds of the garment, as it had fallen to her sides. "He will be gone after two weeks this Friday. You have the number but don't call before then." The door closed gently behind me.

My Friend Henry

I had gone into the rest room at the office to tidy myself and on returning to my desk, Julie came in asking me for the signed receipt, I had received from Mrs Palmer for the documents for the car. For one mad moment I nearly said no I did not have them, to give me the opportunity to go back to collect it. But I thought better of it and reached for my brief case and retrieved it.

The grin on Julie's face told me something was wrong, so I asked what the problem was. "Not a lot." She replied before adding. "It is just that you were a lot longer than expected ... and if you were to remove the lipstick from your neck where the love bite is, then nobody will know it happened very recently, like this morning."

She grinned and thanked me for the receipt and walked away, I was certain she was swaying her hips as she did so. I made another visit to the rest room wondering how I had missed the tell tale mark on my neck on my first visit.

After that brief episode I got more and more involved in my work as it was coming into a busy period. But I was counting the days to the Friday when I could make the phone call and lay with that wonderful form again.

My Friend Henry

Some of my time was taken up with Rob's wedding. As the Best Man I had certain duties before the great day. It was to be held in the little church just off Chadwell Heath High Road with a grand reception on the first floor function room of one of the local pubs.

I think Rob was more surprised, than I was disappointed for not following through and getting in touch with Sally. He did say I had done the right thing and I should get her out of my head. But he knew something, which I didn't.

Chapter Sixteen

The Telephone Box

There was a different atmosphere in the car after the efforts to avoid a nasty accident. Sally had stopped singing and humming to the music.

I suggested stopping "After that near miss and what has just happened, I could use a drink, I don't often drive through closed gates."

Looking across at Sally I was hoping she would agree. To my relief she turned and smiled nodding her head saying "I thought it was your speciality". Well I had to grin at that.

We were going up what was a steep incline, with high banks to each side. The engine in the car had started to sound stressed. I changed down a gear to help it. As we came over the top the view was breath taking...well it would have been if it had not been at night, nevertheless it was still glorious.

My Friend Henry

The vision was enhanced by the lights of a small town spread out before us about two miles away. As we entered the outskirts twin bright lights over the swinging sign with a big cat on it and attached to the wall of a public house declaring it was the Red Lion. It looked like the sort of place we would both enjoy.

There was not much of a car park to one side, in fact it was tiny, just enough space for two cars, one of which had already been taken. I was not certain but it was similar to the car I had seen go past as we had left the diversion we had taken through the closed gate.

I parked the car in the remaining portion. Once Sally was out of the car she held tightly on to my arm as we walked around the corner and into the covered porch of the entrance way.

A little way up the road, on the other side of the Red Lion, I noticed a man with a 'deer stalker' type of hat speaking on a phone in a red telephone kiosk.

It was warm inside after the chilly air of the early evening. The soft lighting suited both of us. There was a fire crackling as it flared over and consuming logs in the grate, improving the atmosphere with the gentle smell of wood burning, creating a comfortable homely feel.

My Friend Henry

There were two other young couples dressed in tweeds, and no doubt from the local farming community, they were standing at one end of the long bar. One of the group was speaking after which they all laughed. We chose two padded bar stools at the opposite end. I helped Sally up to sit on the high seat and sat opposite her.

Leaning on the bar with one elbow I ordered drinks, which were quickly served. I turned and we were sitting facing each other. I could see her face was still white, following the fright in the car, and when I held her hand I could feel her shaking slightly. I was also feeling the same because of what had taken place...but for a few inches we could very well be laying injured in the road.

Henry was taking interest in the closeness of the lady. That was because her lovely legs were touching mine at the knee and her skirt had risen a little.

Her hands were fiddling with her bag and we were both feeling the horror of the event. Looking at her my love and desire was very strong, which only encouraged Henry.

Sally asked if we had far to go and I replied we should be there in another hour. Then she added "You did very

My Friend Henry

well to get us out of what would have been a nasty accident." I just nodded my head not knowing how to answer. We carried on chatting and enjoying the atmosphere and being on our own albeit in a public place. And there was not a chance of her father coming in through the door and whisking her away.

In the back of my mind I was thinking about the accident and was aware I should report it to the Police as soon as possible. I remembered on entering the Pub noticing that there was a telephone box a little way up the road and thinking to myself that before we got going again I should use it and tell the police what had happened. Perhaps by then the man in the hat will have been gone.

She looked so happy and trusting I wanted to hold and kiss her, but this was not the right time or place. Instead I said "Come on drink up, and we will be on our way." She slid off the chair as I was talking as more laughter came from the far end of the room.

I took her arm saying "There is a call box a little way up the road and I think before we go any further I should use it to report what happened." We walked out to the car arm in arm, which was a great feeling although I could still feel the tension in her. We stopped for a

My Friend Henry

while and exchanged kisses. I broke away as Henry was showing interest.

Turning I gently guided her to walk up to the telephone facility. I saw it was still being used by the man wearing that different type of hat. We stood waiting for him to finish but he turned his back to us as if to say this will take some time. So, I decided not to wait any longer and we were soon on our way and looking forward to our arrival and the rest of the evening.

Chapter Seventeen

Rendered Speechless

The wedding between Rob and Wendy was held in March. The arrangement was for the marriage ceremony to be held in the quaint little church, which with its Norman type clock tower was built in the late eighteen hundreds and situated just off the High Road in Chadwell Heath.

Afterwards a reception was planned with dining, singing and dancing. Normally the third month of the year, although the start of Spring, is one in which it can be windy and cold. As it happened the weather forecast was good and the day turned out to be even better, with a warm sun beaming down as if it was giving its approval of the events.

A shining black wedding limo decked out in ribbons and flowers, which had been one part of my duties to organise, arrived outside where the marriage ceremony was to take place.

Three bridesmaids alighted from the car holding coloured posies and stood in a group to one side outside the church to wait for the bride. The planning of this

My Friend Henry

group had nothing to do with me, it had been arranged and organised by the bride's mother.

Rob, a nervous groom, and myself had gone inside the pretty little church shortly before the arrival of the bridal party, so we were out of the way when they arrived; the two of us were with the vicar in the vestry settling his account.

With the paperwork out of the way the three of us moved to stand in the chancel in front of the altar, and waited for the bride to arrive.

Soft organ music played by the resident organist, was wafting through the nave as the guests all dressed elegantly, walked slowly in to take their seats, squeezing into the narrow rows of the pews, where they adjusted cushions and their clothing trying to make themselves comfortable as they sat down.

Others were wearing a little more than the weather required, and were busy removing top clothing in the confined space. There was the soft hum of voices as greetings were exchanged

For a moment I, like most 'best man's,' was a little worried as I had forgotten where I had put the ring and

My Friend Henry

was gently going through my pockets trying to locate it. With a little sigh I felt its familiar shape in my waistcoat pocket, a garment I rarely wore.

Rob looked nervous and probably was, his smile was not the usual relaxed version he normally showed to the world. The wait seemed endless and I think we were both wondering if the bride had changed her mind. The vicar standing tall in his long white cassock was calmness itself, with his hands clasped in front of him, smiling at everyone his eyes sparkling as he looked around him.

It was with some relief when the organist, who had received some form of signal, changed the music from a melody she had been playing to 'Here Comes the Bride.' The congregation who had been murmuring amongst themselves went quiet and with a shuffling noise rose to their feet, and as one, turned to look down the church. Likewise Rob and I did the same.

Wendy, in a long white wedding gown with a veil attached to a small white hat with flowers around the rim, appeared coming through the wide open dark oak door to one side of the church. She was holding onto her father's arm. He was a nice person who I had met a few times and now walking upright and tall he looked splendid dressed in a grey morning suit.

My Friend Henry

They turned into the centre aisle and walked slowly side by side along it towards the altar to where we were standing. As they passed the pews, with a mixture of friends and family on each side of the aisle, they frequently acknowledged those present.

Walking directly behind Wendy were the three bridesmaids in two rows. They were all dressed in long off the shoulder pale yellow dresses holding small bunches of flowers. Immediately behind the bride was her sister and behind her a further pair ... I froze.

The abrupt appearance of the lovely face with the wonderful expression belonging to Sally, made me swallow hard. I stared at those wonderful beautiful features with that stunning smile. I had dreamed of her so many times since I had first seen her all those months ago.

She looked dazzling, relaxed unpretentious and lovely. Sally could light up any room and could turn me to jelly. And now she was looking straight at me with those flashing eyes and the rest of the world became a misty gabble in a swirling mass.

My Friend Henry

That magic feeling of being drawn to her swept over me. An unknown specific inner working of the mind and body, making an invisible connection with Sally. I could feel the pull towards her. Nothing else mattered. It took a lot of will power to turn away and resume with the wedding ceremony. My heart was beating at a faster rate and it was nothing to do with the responsibilities I had to perform that afternoon.

Chapter Eighteen

Two Happy Souls

At long last the ceremony was over, most of the time I had not really comprehended what was going on as my mind was too full of Sally sitting a few feet away.

I also could not understand why I did not know of her being present as I had been involved almost on a daily basis of how the event was to unfold.

The group was making it's way out of the church for the photo call. The two of us, Sally and I, had only a few chances to nod at each other and say 'hello', on the other hand too much was going on for anything further. The smile from those lovely blue eyes sending messages in my direction helped.

I did have a quick word with Rob asking why he hadn't told me Sally was one of the Bridesmaids. He just grinned and said he wanted to surprise me and turned away to speak to someone else.

At the Wedding Breakfast Sally was seated two chairs away from me with the groom's sister, as head bridesmaid, sitting next to me.

My Friend Henry

Finally, the meal was over, and guests were talking and some were getting up from their seats. As if with one thought Sally and I stood up. We smiled at each other and walked closely together away from the table. We were both holding a glass of wine and heading towards a quieter part of the room where we found two chairs to sit down on and to get to know each other.

The afternoon sped past very pleasantly. Sally was excellent company and when not chatting we would stroll onto the small wooden paved area to dance. She was an expert following my moves and all the time smiling and laughing. She told me she had taken lessons and amusingly told me I should when I made a clumsy mistake.

As the time went past we got on well, although in some respects very much still strangers, it was as two people at comfort with each other naturally finding out about our lives. Rob smiled at us and said something about it being obvious we did not need any introduction.

When we first started to talk she admonished me for not getting in touch, and of course she was right in that she had made it obvious at the party that is what she had wanted.

My Friend Henry

I had replied sheepishly, I thought she was involved with Mike, and then I discovered she had only gone out with him to make up a foursome with her friend and had not seen him again. Wonderful words which were so much music to my ears.

We danced and chatted for most of the afternoon, and even Henry knew he wasn't wanted, although he would give a little twitch now and again, just to remind me he was still there. It was great holding her as we danced around the crowded floor feeling her firm soft body swaying to the rhythm.

I made it clear I wanted to see her again, she snuggled up to me and said it would be nice but the earliest she said I could see her was the following Saturday, so we made arrangements for me to go to her home to collect her.
Suddenly she had vanished. I had excused myself, as one does at these sort of affairs, and when I returned to an empty chair where she had been sitting,

I looked at it in amazement and looked around the room to see where she had gone. I was then told she had gone home. I was devastated and now I was not sure if we still had a date. Rob said softly 'Daddy called for her and demanded she leave.'

My Friend Henry

When I did venture to her home hoping the arrangement was still on, her father came to the gate inspecting me and the car and looking at me as if I was scum. Sally was close behind him before passing him and modestly walked around the car, she waved to her parent and joined me inside

Over the coming months a sort of routine set in, I would collect her on the Saturday or Sunday at the weekend and she would be anxious to get home before ten thirty. When we pulled up outside father was always waiting, either at the window or the gate, so there never was time for a cuddle and a good night kiss.

I was not too concerned as Sally was good company and intelligent to talk to. However, there was that feeling between us that something was missing. We both knew, sooner or later if we were to stay seeing each other, then more was needed in the relationship, although Henry knew his place and would show interest now and then, he never got into a state of excitement.

One Saturday evening Sally and I had been dancing. We came out strolling hand in hand and on reaching the car, I had found a place to leave it in a car park behind the cinema not very far from the dance hall.

My Friend Henry

At the time it had been almost full. Now it was deserted, and the car stood forlornly on its own and waiting in a dark corner of the available space.

After unlocking it, I paused and looked at her. She looked lovely. Behind her a distant streetlight was framing her in its glow. Sally understood what I wanted. She smiled and looked at the rear door. I did not need to say anything further and feeling a need flashing through me I opened the back.

Sally looked at me and smiled before sliding onto the back seat her skirt and the slips riding up her legs. I joined her and we fell into each other's arms. It was the first time we had really kissed passionately.

My hand pushed her skirt higher. Suddenly she went stiff and pushed my hand away. Murmuring "Not now." We started kissing again, my heart was pounding, and I was breathing in short breaths. It was a little while later when we parted company and made our way home, both of us feeling the intensity and passion of being together and yet knowing there was something missing.

Chapter Nineteen

The Affair

After the event in the car park Sally kept her distance, although over the coming months we got very passionate however she would not allow us to do anything extra. It was not enough, and I was feeling more and more frustrated and wanted to go further, on occasions I was a little bad tempered.

I had not been in touch with Mrs Palmer; the notion had not entered my head as Sally occupied my thoughts and longings. Nevertheless, as time went by the consideration grew on me to phone her.

I mulled over it for some time and then one weekend I was told Sally was going away on a family holiday for three weeks. After which I felt lonely and the temptation to pick up the telephone on the following morning was very strong.

I was not certain if Mr Palmer was away or not and it was with trepidation, I dialled her number, ready to put the phone down if he answered. The husky voice over the line made me feel warm inside especially when she sounded pleased to hear from me. On meeting the lady later that day Mrs Palmer put on a little sulk because I

My Friend Henry

had not been in touch for some time however, she knew how to keep Henry happy.

We settled into a routine again when her husband was away, we would meet once or twice a week, but never at her home like the first time, normally in a motel. On entering the room she would quickly strip her clothes off and wait to be pleasured.

She had this way of locking Henry inside her demanding everything. In some ways, although feeling guilty when Sally and I met, the need in me was absent and the time together was more pleasant as I had no need to pressure her.

Months went by and my life seemed perfect. I enjoyed my work and other leisure activities and Mrs Palmer was still being very active when we met.

It was at the end of the summer when she told me the Professor was going away for an extended period. We started to meet more frequently and although rewarding and enjoyable it was not enough and was not what I wanted, as Sally dominated my thoughts.

It was a strange mixed feeling, making the arrangement to see her and then not wanting to go ... but when with

My Friend Henry

her, the sheer joy of being together overcame the previous thoughts.

As the weeks and months drifted past we were both tired of the routine and started to find an excuse for not meeting. A little later, just before Christmas, I saw her in the High Street holding another man's hand and it was not her husband. For some reason I felt very jealous and yet I knew the relationship would come to an end, but the feelings for her didn't and in the back of my mind I knew at some time I would see her again.

Without the clandestine affair with Mrs Palmer I wanted more than Sally was prepared to give. The weekends when we got together continued and on occasion during the week if there was something special on. But it was more like a brother and sister arrangement except on the odd occasion we would hold each other passionately.

Chapter Twenty

Temptation

When enjoying one's existence without the need to worry about the future, time disappears in a meaningless rush. It was the second year of knowing the lovely Sally, although very little had changed, and our time together was still very limited.

We were in our favourite dance hall one Saturday evening. I had gone to the bar to refresh our drinks. I felt a touch on my shoulders and turned. My old girlfriend Eileen was smiling at me. "Hello Dennis...I thought I may find you here!"

By the time I had looked her up and down at the skimpy outfit she was wearing; the barman had given up waiting for my order and had gone elsewhere.

I looked into the face I knew so well. For some reason she looked younger, perhaps it was the makeup. She was certainly dressed for the part with a low neckline and her perfume drifted over me.

I was a little taken aback and for some reason I could not think of what to say. It was nice to see her again, as we had not fallen out when we had parted company, I

My Friend Henry

guess at the time we had just been tired of what was becoming a tedious habit and needed something or someone fresh.

Eileen had made it very clear, in the days when I was available, settling down was not in her plan. She was much a career woman with a high-power job, and she saw men as play things and she was good at it.

I was pleased to see her, and I smiled, not knowing what to say I nodded my head and said "Yes! Most weekends...you are looking lovely...are you here with someone?" The words tumbled out of me and I realised I was a little tongue tied with my pulse going up a notch or two.

"He's a bit of a bore and sitting over there." She nodded in the direction that she was talking of "We don't normally come here but I heard this is where you are on a Saturday night...so I convinced him to bring me along so I could see you."

I swallowed hard and even Henry started to take notice of the conversation. While I enjoyed Sally's company we had got into a rut and there was no excitement between us. There was also the problem of her family, her father

My Friend Henry

was so demanding and his reluctance to allow a serious relationship, also her mother was not much help.

Although we had from time to time spoken of a more permanent relationship there was no enthusiasm from her parents for it.

I found myself saying "What have you got in mind?" then having said it, I felt uncomfortable because it really meant I was agreeing to arrange to meet her.

She smiled and looked over her shoulder to where her current date was sitting. Turning back to me she went all coy and modest but having known her for some time I realised she was up to something.

By now we had had time to order drinks and had been served. Picking up the gin and tonic, for some reason it felt so familiar seeing her sip it as I had seen her do something similar many times in the past.

I wasn't certain if she was laughing or just smiling when she said "I thought you would like to join my darts team?"

I was a regular player with a darts team, so it raised my interest. I shrugged my shoulders "Why not? Where do

My Friend Henry

you play?" she was smiling when she said the White Horse. Being a person familiar with most Pubs I knew they did not have a darts team and also knowing the premises I could not see where the room was for a dart board. So I looked at her quizzically asking "I did not know they had a darts team ... who else is in it?"

She glanced towards Sally before saying "Oh, just you and me!" Looking back at me with a big grin on her face Eileen continued "We can develop a new game played only just by two."

Henry got interested as obviously it wasn't darts she had in mind. She said "Why don't we play on Wednesday evening, as I remember you get off early on that day." Eileen continued as she collected her drink saying "About seven then ... why don't you collect me and we can go together." And then she abruptly walked away swinging her hips in an exaggerated way.

I returned to Sally feeling a little flushed, also guilty. Before I reached where she was sitting I could see the daggers in her eyes which were not as sparkling with the lowering of her lids. The rest of the evening was a bit frosty and I did not know how to break the tension.

My Friend Henry

We had a habit of kissing good night when we got in the car as it was not possible to have a cuddle when I took her home...but never in the back seat a second time. This time she seemed to be a bit more passionate.

Chapter Twenty One

Embarrassing

Wednesday. For most of the day I had been in a quandary as I had spent the afternoon fighting with my principles to meet Eileen or not. I tried to phone Sally to see if I could see her that evening only to be told sharply she was going out with her parents.

I put the phone down and as her mother had not been forthcoming where she was going, I was a little annoyed.

My Friend Henry

The evening was approaching and I had to make a decision.

On leaving the car site, as I drove home I was in turmoil as my opinion was 'after all the months Sally and I had been together, one would have thought I would have also been invited out with the family'. I learned at the weekend they had gone to see a show in the West End of London.

It was after six and I was hesitating whilst enjoying a sandwich when I finally made up my mind to go and join Eileen's darts team, but I had a feeling darts would not come into it.

After a quick shave and change into smart casual clothing I was on my way. She was a master, or should that be mistress, for she knew how to make a man interested, as when I arrived outside her handsome detached house with her late Jaguar in the driveway, she posed in the frame of the front door, with the light behind her showing off the shape of her body. As a wealthy individual in her own right I could not help seeing an image of her in my mind of her dressed in her day wear of a smart business suit.

My Friend Henry

I had to grin to myself and when I saw she wasn't exactly dressed for playing darts my guess was if she started to try and throw an arrow her scanty covering of a top would have difficulty in keeping everything in place. I wondered what she had in mind and I had a feeling we, that is Henry and me, were going to like it.

The White Horse was a turning to the right, but she told me to turn left. I looked at her a little puzzled but said nothing. Pointing a hand with coloured manicured nails she directed me to the main road and then another turn and we were heading out of town. Although still not certain where we were going, I followed instructions. Eventually I said, "You did not mean the local White Horse, did you?" I had suspicions she just meant Whites, a motel and we were heading in that direction.

She grinned and nodded her head and turning to look at me with a broad smile, her very white teeth glistening in the fading light. "I just had a feeling I wanted to see you again...for old time's sake."

She shrugged as she said "The 'horse' part just slipped out!" Eileen was still looking at me and continued smiling as she reached across and rubbed my knee. Henry suddenly started to feel different and I could feel him throbbing. Sexual games with her were always different,

My Friend Henry

two never the same as she would find different ways for us to enjoy each other.

Weeks were to pass and the two of us, that is Eileen and I, were becoming very familiar with the hotels and motels around the district as the Wednesday night became something special. However, after a period of time, and spending the regular weekly meetings with the sex bomb it all became a little meaningless.

Henry was happy...but I wasn't! Because the only person I really wanted to be with, was Sally, and for a time I had felt the two of us were drifting apart. But somehow, I could not bring the Wednesday arrangement to a close.

One evening we were again visiting Whites and as usual, as a way of relaxing before the evenings event, we were sitting in the bar enjoying a drink, me with my beloved Scotch whisky whilst Eileen always had a Gin and Tonic, pink of course.

She was dressed in another daring outfit with her legs in high heeled soft leather boots with a very short skirt way above the knee with the shadow between her closed legs giving a hint of excitement. The matching top

My Friend Henry

seemingly finishing before it had started. I had my favourite chequered jacket on with grey trousers.

There was some kind of function taking place in the large room just past where we were sitting, which catered for weddings and other similar occasions.

People in their evening attire, ladies in long dresses and the men with black bow ties, were starting to make their way to the event they were attending.

Some had their arms linked, all laughing, chatting and smiling as they slowly went past in the passageway, there was glass panelling separating the bar where we were sitting, from the walkway.

I was relaxed in the chair admiring Eileen and wondering what games she was going to play this evening.

I was side on to the people parading past; nonetheless I could see them in the reflection of the mirror fixed to the shelves behind the bar.

Still contemplating the pleasures of the late afternoon when I turned my head and Sally dressed beautifully in a long pinkish gown was walking past the door with her father and mother. But who was the fellow? I had no

My Friend Henry

idea who he was, I didn't think it was her brother. Even though Sally was looking straight ahead I was not certain, but I felt as if she had seen me.

The evening lost its lustre. Eileen smiled at me saying "She looked this way, but I don't think she saw you. If she did, I am no threat, I am content and married to my work. The two of you will eventually get married and be happy together."

She had gone a little serious and fiddled with the glass. "Anyway ... I will always be happy to see you and a phone call away." She had said it in a sad way as if it was not what she wanted.

I looked at her differently, somehow the thought of going to the bedroom with her had changed. It was a sobering thought.

Anyway, we both knew she was no threat, but did Sally know that? However, as much as the excitement had left me Henry needed to have his way and a little time later with a heavy heart, I followed her. When we arrived in the bedroom, I was worried about leaving and finding Sally and family waiting for me in the foyer. After a brief encounter as neither of us were in the mood, we left earlier than usual.

My Friend Henry

The following weekends arrangements were cancelled. I received a brief telephone call from Sally's mother saying that she was not well and was confined to her bed. I did not know what to think. I was certain she had seen me during the week and had decided not to see me again.

Three weeks were to pass and despite trying to get in touch with her at her home and place of work, I did not manage to talk to her.

It was Monday morning and as usual I was walking up and down the car site, trying to keep busy and also out of the cold wind. The bell on the wall of the office started to clanger.

Julie as usual answered the phone and then called me from the small balcony surrounding the offices that the call was for me. To my surprise it was Sally. She sounded upset and then she told me "I have told my father he has got to let me run my own life and if you are willing I would like you to take me away this weekend." The words came rushing out without a pause and that is why we are in the car going down to Devon.

Chapter Twenty Two

Confinement

I am now sitting on a hard bench looking at four white tiled walls and with nothing else to do I started contemplating that some journeys are trouble-free with no holdups, others especially if you are in a hurry, are one delay after another.

I am sure the reader knows the feeling of when one is late for work because you had forgotten to set the alarm clock the evening before, and you had not woken up in time. Then in a hurry with a slice of toast in one hand while you struggle to unlock the door to the car, only to find it won't start.

You watch the clock on the dashboard creeping round while pressing the starter listening to the engine turning over but not firing, hoping as you continue to press the button that the battery will hold up. When the motor

My Friend Henry

comes to life and you are on your way every other delay will slow your progress making you later than ever.

This journey had been one of those times; delay after delay, what was supposed to be an exciting leisurely journey had become a serious expedition.

The first hold up had been when at the time we had intended to start out, we were delayed because Sally had some sort of problem in her office, which had to be resolved first.

After we were finally on our way, I was told we had to go back. From a man's point of view the item left behind was of little importance.

Finally, after more than an hour from the time we had planned, we were on our way. Then the traffic had seemed, no not seemed, was far heavier than normal.

The real frustration ... virtually every set of traffic light we approached turned to red forcing us to stop. Then the wait for the duration of the system, before they turned to green and allowed us to proceed.

My Friend Henry

Normally by now, considering the time we had left London we should have been well on our way, if not there.

And of course our real problems started when I looked away from where we were going to adjust the heating control in the car ... well the lady had said her feet were cold. It was a new model of the famous mark and as a result the layout of the controls had been changed, which meant I needed to see where they were before I could adjust them.

If I hadn't looked away from where we were going then I would have seen the other car coming straight for us. Although it would have been difficult to avoid it but if that had been the case then I would have had far more room and could have dealt with the situation more comfortably.

Thinking about it now that five bar gate was the real start of our troubles. Although in some ways it had saved us from a nasty accident when we ploughed through it. Now it was going to have the last laugh as it was the cause of all our difficulty.

As I continued to sit on the hard seat with a poor excuse for a cushion come sleeping mattress, I was

My Friend Henry

thinking back on what happened next on that fateful journey. Alright not quite fateful, but it was in destroying what was supposed to have been a wonderful weekend.

When I turned the car round in the field, and I saw another car go past at the time I thought little of it.

Even when we had stopped at the pub to get over the event, there had been a chance to solve the problem as on leaving we saw the man in the telephone kiosk. He was talking on the phone with an unusual type of hat perched on the back of his head.

How was I to know when I thought he was of no concern to us, and yet he was the one who would be the problem.

If I had not been so keen to get on our way and had approached him explaining what had happened, maybe I would not be sitting in this cell. But then again I did not know at the time who he was.

A little after departing the quaint little hostelry where we had stopped for a drink, I noticed the engine's temperature gauge had started to edge upwards. I had an awful feeling that when we crashed through the gate it had damaged the radiator on the front of the car.

My Friend Henry

I kept on going hoping nothing too serious had happened to it, and drove on a little further only to watch the temperature reading getting dangerously high, so I had pulled into the side of the road.

Sally looked with surprise in my direction. I smiled and shrugged my shoulders, saying "I need to look under the bonnet" as I dragged the hand brake on and pulled the lever so I could open it. She had replied, "What's wrong ... is it serious?"

I had my fingers crossed when I replied "Hopefully ... no, I won't be too long." As I had got out of the car and walking round it I was wondering if this journey was ever going to end. I could hear the hissing before seeing it.

It was a serious problem! However, I also knew how to keep us mobile and that was to ease the water pressure in the unit before the water vanished through the damaged part. I knew it should work as it was a very small leak being made larger by the force of the water.

Lifting the bonnet of the car, I had loosened the cap on the head of the radiator with caution, knowing there would be a jet of extremely hot steam, which if not careful would hurt. It worked; the hissing stopped.

My Friend Henry

As we resumed the journey there was now a need to reduce the speed and where possible free wheel downhill taking the strain off the engine to reduce the build-up of heat.

One of the first things that stopped working was the heater, so another stop to get a blanket out of the boot to wrap around Sally's feet. By now I was tired of the journey and was wondering if there would be any energy left in me, or the inclination to do anything, when we finally got to the cottage.

At the gentle pace we were going the journey became boring. Both of us had started to settle down, we had the whole weekend in front of us and we felt good. I turned the music up and as we travelled along, we were singing or humming to the music, and laughing at silly little jokes and innuendoes.

At first when I saw the blue flashing light behind me I did not think anything of it. Why should I. We were not going very fast, I was very sober and the thought of the event earlier in the evening, whilst not forgotten was not important. It appeared they were in a hurry so I was looking for a place where we could move over and give them space.

Chapter Twenty Three

The Hat

It was such a beautiful evening, although dark the sky was clear and the stars playing around in the heavens. It was just perfect and at last we were making headway and having fun and totally relaxed. The other car behind us seemed to settle down and although unsettling it did not really trouble me.

As I said, at first I thought the Police Car wanted to go past. We were approaching a portion of the road which was wider than the part we had been travelling on. I slowed, put on the left hand flasher and pulled over to give him room. But he didn't and he stayed behind us flashing his head lights.

Suddenly I felt nervous and continued driving, until a lay-by sign appeared. Once more I indicated that we would pull into it. Well I had wanted to stop in one earlier but not for the same reason.

As we came to a stop Sally looked at me "Why are the Police stopping us?" I looked at her shrugging my shoulders and grinned as a way of reply hoping to show I was not too concerned.

My Friend Henry

But I was. There was a funny guilt feeling in me which I could not understand. Winding the window down and watching in the mirrors the policeman walking towards us, then I noticed the chevrons on his arms and realised he was a Sergeant and thought 'Do Sergeants do traffic patrol?'

He bent over and looked in the window "Good evening Sir...do you know why we stopped you?"

Well I thought 'The Sir' was a good start.' My answer "No officer, I know I wasn't speeding!" His pleasant manner was spoilt, and so was the Sir bit, because he leaned through the window and turning the engine off he took the keys from the ignition.

Opening the door he asked me to step outside, saying "The lady is to stay in the car".

I started to feel a little aggrieved and wanted to demand why he had stopped us but being polite in front of traffic policemen is always the best way of thinking. Nevertheless, I could not understand why he had taken the car keys and had the feeling there was more to this than he was saying.

My Friend Henry

We stood facing each other, with my thoughts whirling around in my head and he with a big grin on his face, I started to think this was someone's idea of a joke. "What is your name?" he demanded in a gentle yet firm voice in which I sensed a hidden meaning.

I replied "Dennis Walker." I thought it was best to humour him and not to be too difficult and then perhaps we could be on our way. He had taken a note book out of his pocket and was writing in it, which I guessed was my name. Then he asked for my driving license. I felt a little hot under the collar as I told him I did not have it.

He nodded his head as if he understood and then asked where it was. "I'm sorry officer, I forgot to pick it up, it is in the drawer in my office desk."

He looked at me and the grin seemed to be getting larger. "Useful place desk draws are, no doubt you frequently get stopped by the Police when you are driving your desk!" His eyes were twinkling and grinning.

Once more he was looking back up the road where we had come from. He had done this a few times since stopping us. I had the feeling there was more to it than just looking. He would also glance at the front of the car

My Friend Henry

where there was slight damage which was caused when we hit the gate.

"Okay Sir! I suppose there is no need for me to ask for your Motor Insurance for no doubt that is also in the office desk?" I sheepishly nodded my head. "This shouldn't be too difficult, where have you come from?"

"We have just driven down from London on our way to Devon for the weekend. We have been delayed as I expected to be there by now."

He wrote something in the notebook before he had another quick look back up the road before saying, still with that grin on his face "Is that your wife in the car?" I shook my head adding "No ... I'm not married." I could have hit him when he said "Oh! So you are on the way for a naughty weekend." He scribbled something in the notebook.

"Does your wife...sorry, girlfriend drive?" I shook my head. "So, you have driven all the way?"

By now I was starting to feel a little impatient, but I tried to stay calm as I did not want to upset him. "Yes, since we have left." Then he wanted to know if I had

My Friend Henry

been drinking. I nodded my head I added "just a quick one".

I could hear another car coming and as it came into sight, I had the feeling it was the one that drove past as we exited from the field, after going through the closed gate. It pulled up behind the police car.

An elderly gentleman wearing a deer stalker type of hat got out. He was waving a short stick in the air saying very loudly "Ha ... you caught the scoundrel ... well done officer"

I immediately recognised him as the person who was wearing that head gear and had been talking on the phone in the telephone kiosk when we had stopped for a drink.

I watched and was fascinated as he approached the Police Sergeant with firm steps, the bushy hair on his upper lip bristling in the breeze and bouncing up and down keeping in time with his mouth and loud voice.

Pointing to our car he said, "That is the vehicle Officer, which recklessly drove through my closed gate onto my land churning up the grass and damaging the gate beyond repair!"

My Friend Henry

The Sergeant looked away from me and turning asked him if he was certain that it was me and how did he recognise the car.

"I live not fifty yards from my gate ... which is now useless ... and had just arrived home and was getting out of my car when I heard the bang, I immediately got back in the car and was in time to see him, (pointing at me) driving out of the gate"

"So Sir, you are certain that this gentlemen was responsible for destroying your gate?"

"If he was driving that bloody thing - pointing at the car - then it was him who rashly and dangerously drove through my closed gate destroying it." Suddenly I felt uncomfortable with a feeling of hopelessness.

The Police Sergeant turned to me and addressing me with my surname said he was arresting me for criminal damage of destroying the gate of the Land Owner. Also for not stopping at the scene of an accident. Not reporting a road accident. Also dangerous driving and doing so while under the influence of alcohol. With a sickly smirk he added did I have anything to say.

My Friend Henry

I looked at him in shock and at first I wanted to laugh. I was now convinced it was a wind up by the lads who I worked with at the car site.

Then I realised the truth, I had crashed through the gate. I knew he was serious when he took hold of my arms and clipped handcuffs on my wrist. I tried to explain what had happened, but it was no use, he just grinned and said save it for the Magistrate. I was bundled into the back of the police vehicle. Although with a big beam on his face he did apologise for destroying my weekend. The thought crossed my mind if you are going to go through a stranger's gate then pick one that is open.

Chapter Twenty Four

Abandoned

At the police station Mr Deerstalker, still wearing that head gear as if it was some form of trophy, was listening to the proceedings while some of the time grinning although that would quickly turn into a frown.

It was here I learned the gate we destroyed was owned by the local landowner, him with the hat, who had a lot of influence with the Local Authority and hence the law enforcement.

Sally was brought in by another policeman accompanied by a policewoman and had been told to sit down a little way from me. She was only there for a brief moment before she was escorted into another room, but before being ushered away, she caught my eye and then asked me to tell her what it was all about. I did not know how to reply and said it was something to do with the accident when we went through the gate.

Behind a high desk there was a burly Police Sergeant looking down at me and surrounded by different types of files and thick ledgers. One of which he had taken down from a shelf and opened it on the desk to a new page, with different types of headings on it. He asked for my name date of birth and where I lived in a

My Friend Henry

monotone voice, which doubtless he had used when asking the questions to others many times before.

I tried to explain what had happened and I could see by the look on his face he was not listening, instead he read out the charges of criminal damage and dangerous driving. They had dropped any idea of me being drunk in charge after a brief examination, which came as some relief for me.

Once more I tried to explain that there was no way that I could report the accident as there was no communications available. The man in the hat was determined to make the situation worse for me and told them about the phone box outside the pub.

The policeman behind the desk decided he would let the Magistrates decide if it was an offence. However, they dropped the charge of not staying by an accident when I said it was pointless staying at the time of the mishap as it was in a deserted area. I had used the word 'mishap' as it did not sound so damaging.

Getting a little desperate as I did not want to spend the weekend in the police station, I made it clear I was prepared to pay for the gate. If Mr 'Deerstalker' would accept that and drop the complaint then that would only

My Friend Henry

leave the dangerous driving charge, and the other weak one of not reporting an accident.

Quite frankly I could not see how they could make either of them stick, as surely with Sally as a witness to what had happened there could be no allegation to answer.
The policeman was looking totally bored and he also had a habit of scratching one ear as he made an entry in the ledger. In the meantime I was standing in this draughty reception area on tender hooks wondering what was going to happen, and hoping the offer of paying for the damage would solve the problem. In my mind I was sure my insurers would meet the cost. The phone rang and totally ignoring us, the desk officer listened into it for a brief period and then left the office.

While the Sergeant was absent I turned to Mr 'Hat' and asking him politely if he would change his mind. I saw it as a way of pleading with the only person who was making the complaint to drop the charges. I was feeling certain without his input the Police, with Sally's testimony about what happened, would not proceed.

He looked out of the window as if I did not exist. It did not help matters as I lost my cool for a moment although it made him turn around and look at me only to

My Friend Henry

say I was to be careful otherwise he would add using insulting language to the complaint.

Perhaps instead of being angry with him and I had pleaded instead, things may have been different. The Sergeant came back to his seat with a steaming mug of some beverage in his hand. He looked over at the person with the grievance and said "Do you wish to continue with the complaint, Sir?"

He nodded his head saying "Of course I do!" and instantly walked over to the desk where he was told to sign the entry in the ledger.

I looked on, feeling desperate hoping he would change his mind. He didn't. He turned and before leaving he looked me in the eye and said, "I do not agree with two people of the opposite sex going away together for a weekend when they are not married."

I could not help wondering if I had been less angry and more pleasant, and I was with a man instead of a beautiful lady, he would have been more lenient.

I was told that as I had no documentation with me to prove who I was, I would have to stay the night as their

My Friend Henry

guest in one of their cells before appearing in front of the magistrates.

At first the indication was I would be taken to the place for the hearing the following morning for a special Saturday sitting. However when the time arrived I was told the court could not sit and I would have to wait until Monday, my heart sank as I realised I would have to put up with the decision, and making a mental note to always carry my driving license.

And that is why I am sitting on this hard seat and some form of bed looking at the white tiled walls of the cell which will be my home for the weekend.

Chapter Twenty Five

The Solicitor

After two uncomfortable nights on what was a very hard surface called a bed, and with my sleep being interrupted every half an hour by someone peering at me through a slot in the door, Monday morning arrived.

During my stay the food was awful, although, and providing I paid, one of the constables would go out to the local takeaway, but in reality, I wasn't really hungry. The only relief from the boredom was when I was escorted to a small room where another Officer took a statement from me, which he wrote down in neat handwriting. He stopped every now and again and looked up at me to clarify a point.

My thoughts during this period had been with my girlfriend. When I asked where Sally was, I was told she had decided to go home and had taken a taxi to the railway station, and would have been in time for the last train.

I thought great, 'here am I stuck in a police station and she leaves me to my fate.' But how was she going to explain all this to her family, especially her father, when she would need picking up when she finally reached London.

I was devastated when I learned a lot later she had been told by the police I would probably get a custodial sentence and it was pointless her staying.

On Monday morning a short ride in a police van where we arrived at a very old tall red brick Victorian building with a large clock on the fascia and a sign saying it was where the court sat. I was taken around the back, they removed the hand cuffs and ushered me inside.

I felt scruffy and unshaven with a crumpled shirt, if I was going to appear in front of everyone then I would have preferred to have been ready, tidy and decently dressed.

I had throughout the period frequently asked to speak to a solicitor without a result. Now at last my request was being attended to as I was introduced to the Duty Legal Person, a slim shabby looking youth in a crumbled grey suit in need of pressing, whom I was assured was a very experienced person in these matters. I had my doubts.

My Friend Henry

We sat down at a table in a unkempt room, off to one side of the corridor, on which he laid a bulky brief case. He was fiddling around with some papers and without looking at me asked if I was prepared to allow him to act on my behalf. After confirming I was, he put down the paper he had been studying and asked me to tell him my story. With sad looking eyes, which gave the message that he had listened to similar situations, he did not interrupt although he occasionally nodded his head.

I say he listened, but he seemed to be more interested in what was going on around us as he would frequently look through the open door.

When I pointed out my girlfriend had been allowed to go home instead of being here to tell her side of the story, which would no doubt agree with what I have got to say. He ruffled through his brief case and subtracting a file from many others he looked through it, nodding his head, before saying "I see, this is her statement ... I retrieved it from the police a little while ago." I didn't change my mind about him, but I was a little impressed.

He had closed the file and sat there thinking; all I wanted to do was grab hold of him and shake him up to see if I could get some enthusiasm from him. Still

My Friend Henry

nodding his head he got up and he walked away while I resumed a seat in the passageway.

I could not understand where he had gone. Then I saw him through the crowd of people who were gathered together in the hallway, no doubt relaying to him why they had come to the premises for one reason or another to answer some charge.

I had plenty of time so I watched him as he moved away from them and then stopped at the end of the walkway and started speaking to a group of men.

My mind kept thinking of what should have been a wonderful weekend together with Sally without a care in the world. By now we would be on our way home having explored the delights of each other.

Instead I was worrying what was going to happen when the man with the 'deer stalker hat' was standing in front of the Magistrates and starting to bemoan the loss of his gate because I had driven through it, when closed.

I also had another possibly more serious problem, how was I going to explain to my manager the damage to the car and why I was not at work this coming afternoon, he

My Friend Henry

had not sounded too pleased when I was allowed to phone him on Saturday morning.

The day dragged on and I could do with a cup of tea, but there were no facilities for one although across the road there was the welcome sign of a cafe, which was not of any use as I was not allowed to leave the premises which I was told very firmly by one of the policemen who had been accompanying me.

I was seated on a hard chair and I guess it was because I had not had much sleep the previous two nights that out of boredom my head fell against the wall and I dozed off. Only to be awoken by my name being called and the constable was shaking me.

As I groggily stood up I was shown by a smartly dressed person, who was some form of official to the closed entrance to the Court Room where I was told to stand and stay in one spot until I was wanted.

So, I stood tired and weary just outside the large double wooden doors leading into the interior of the Court. There were a few others in front of me awaiting their fate and it did not help when one of them said the Magistrate on duty was very strict ... so I remained wondering what my fate would be for a stupid accident.

My Friend Henry

An event that I would remember for ever also about not taking my eyes off the road, keeping feet warm and having my drivers license with me..

One by one the others were called in to face the result of the problem they had, some came out smiling, others with long faces, while there were some who did not reappear at all, perhaps taken to the cells as the court went about its business and made a decision on the individual cases.

My little Solicitor, who was supposed to be representing me, appeared standing next to me without saying a word. He was consulting some paper in his hand with his face as long as ever. I was certain his cheeks would crack if he tried to smile.

He looked up but not at me as his eyes were wandering around as if he was expecting someone. My expectation and curiosity were finally satisfied when he turned to me mumbling something like "You will be called shortly, follow the usher and I'll put your defence after the formalities." Suddenly he was gone.

Chapter Twenty Six

Three Wise Individuals

The sombre atmosphere in the Court Room enveloped me like a cloud. Every noise appeared to echo around the room with my footsteps clip clopping above it as everyone's eyes swivelled in my direction.

Behind the tall bench at one end two men and a woman sat looking down at me, and on the far side of the room I could see the gent who had made the complaint but without having his head gear on. To his left on a stand stood the Police Sergeant who had arrested me, still grinning at me as I was instructed to go to my place.

I was shown into a small wooden pen with no seat and after repeating my name and address I was told to hold a bible in my right hand and to repeat the blurb the usher was chanting.

As I just said there were three elderly people sitting behind the tall bench. On the left was a smartly dressed mature woman in lilac, with grey curly hair framing her face which was masked in thick rimmed black framed eyeglasses. She looked over at me as if I was something the dog had brought in.

On the right a small skinny little man with thin hair on his head a small strand of which was struggling loose over his forehead, as if it was trying to escape from the remainder. He was leaning forward hardly appearing over the top of the desk and seemed

My Friend Henry

to be more interested in scribbling things on some pad and hardly looked up, and when he did it was at the ceiling and with total boredom.

The mature man in the centre was also smartly dressed in a navy blue suit. He had a totally bald head with not a strand in sight and the lighting from the ceiling reflecting from the shiny top. He was wearing small silver framed glasses perched on the end of his nose, which he looked over to study me as I was paraded down through the court room to my position.

My little man of a solicitor was sitting down in the well of the court. He stood up and started to address the bench. The Magistrate in the middle held his hand up flat and with a strike from left to right cutting him off. My representative nodded his head and sat down. I thought 'what was going on, he was supposed to be looking after me, and there he was at the first hurdle giving up.'

The three Magistrates leaned over in a huddle. Although the little man on the right did not get any further than the broad back of the one in the middle and was leaning on the desk to try and peer round him. The bulky one in the middle was leaning towards the lady on his right where he was inches away from her bosom.

They were talking in low whispers and nodding their heads. With my heart beating faster and my fingers crossed, I watched as they continued conversing in low tones whilst occasionally, they would look in my direction. Eventually they sat up and resumed their postures.

My Friend Henry

Peering down at my little man the head Magistrate, well I assumed he was the head as he was sitting in the middle, looked at him and asked if he was the council for the defence. I thought 'what a waste of time, he had already told him he was when he was told to sit down.'

The Solicitor seemed to unwind from the chair as he stood up saying he was, as he did, he was nodding his head at the same time. And then in a strong voice, which surprised me he said, "Your Honour." He said it as if he did not believe in the word. "My client has an unblemished history..."

From the bench the man in the centre waved his arms in a slicing movement again also saying that it was enough. I thought 'Enough? He had hardly said anything, and perhaps I would have a chance to speak before they passed sentence, and I had a lot to say.' He, the Magistrate, then seemed to think about it and added "Is there anything else you want tell to the Court?"

My solicitor, who had sat down again after being told to shut up, stood up this time in the lazy sort of way he did everything. "Your Honour, having looked through the evidence, I do not understand why my client is in this Court answering charges which should not exist..." Following this statement a murmur from those in the Public Gallery went round the court room.

Once again much to my frustration he was told to shut up, and I am thinking what sort of court is this. The Magistrate turned towards the policeman "Constable..." He was interrupted by the Officer saying, "Sergeant ... your Honour."

My Friend Henry

"Yes...yes. Sergeant...have you anything to say? He glared at him over the top of his glasses his eyes firing daggers, daring him to say something, I almost laughed. And then to my delight the Sergeant said, "No sir!"

The Magistrates as one, looked in my direction and all three had a smile on their faces, especially the woman who was looking at me as my mother used to when I had been naughty, but she understood why.

The one in the middle looked down at some papers and took a deep breath before saying "Mr Walker, we are appalled this matter ever came to be in front of this Court. We have read the statement given by your witness and it is obvious to us there is no charge to be answered concerning 'Dangerous Driving' and we do not understand, and I reiterate, why it was ever brought before us. So, on that matter the case is dismissed."

A further murmur went round the court as if everyone agreed to the finding, even my little man who was studying his files again gave a little grin.

The Magistrate continued. "According to the advice that has been given to us, there is another nonsense on the charge sheet." He looked up with that daring look again, waiting for someone to contradict him, when that did not happen he continued. "And that is 'Not Reporting the Accident.' The bench is well aware of where the accident took place and we agree with the defendant's statement that he did not have an opportunity to report it because the Police had arrested him."

My Friend Henry

With a sigh of relief, I thought that is two problems out of the way, and crossing my fingers again I waited while his Honour looked down at some papers on his desk and turning the page before he looked up again. "Now there is the matter of 'Criminal Damage!'" He looked down again and the dramatics of his actions flooded through the Court Room. I held my breath.

"Once more we have taken advice on this matter..." indicating the other two before continuing "we do not understand how this charge of 'Criminal Damage' was ever brought before this Court." He paused and with further theatrical actions he looked around the room.

The little man on his right was busy looking at something on the desk brushing the wayward hair lock out of his eyes. Whilst the 'Lady', while looking and surveying the Court, was nodding her head. As there was no response once more, he looked down at his papers and continued,

"We understand there was the destruction of the five bar gate..." He stopped and leaning forward across the high bench he looked down at the Clerk of the Court sitting in front of the tall desk.

With a puzzled look on his face "What is a 'five bar gate' Clerk is it some form of drinking establishment?" There was brief laughter from the spectators. The recipient of the question shook his head and murmured something before turning and bowing his head and spoke in a whisper to the others near him.

My Friend Henry

There was silence in the Court Room, although someone giggled again.

"Your Honour, I am informed ... and with respect your Honour, it is a device normally used by farmers to enclose a wide opening to a field and the name derives from the way they are constructed with five horizontal wooden bars." This caused more giggling and laughter in the Court Room.

His Honour was nodding his head and banging his gavel to quieten the noise, while the 'Lady in Lilac' grinned and the other was busy pushing the strand of hair out of his eyes again and looking up at the ceiling as if it was important.

The head of the magistrates said, "Thank you Clerk ... of course I knew what we were referring to, but it was important that everyone in this Court understood what a 'five bar gate' was." He said huffily. I was impatient to know where the proceedings were going and was relieved when he turned his attention back to me.

He hesitated and referred to the document in front of him and then looked at his colleagues, where they had a quick discussion with the lady first then the other who suddenly seemed to take interest, before he returned his attention back to me and continued.

"Mr Walker, as I was saying we do not understand why so much time has been wasted to bring you before this Court to answer a charge of Criminal Damage, to this ah, ah ... that gate with the

---

My Friend Henry

bars." He said it as if the 'bar' was important and he could not wait to go to one.

At that there was further giggling in the room. He looked around at everyone as if scolding them with his eyes before turning back to me and resuming. "We also understand you have made it known to the owner that you are prepared to pay for the damage, which was caused by the accident previously mentioned when you were charged with dangerous driving a charge which this Court has dismissed."

For one brief moment he glared across the Court Room at the landowner before continuing. "We have come to the conclusion there is no charge to answer and our understanding is you have been put to a great amount of inconvenience and we award you one hundred pounds to be paid out of Public Funds. You may leave this court without a stain on your character." The other two Magistrates were nodding their heads in agreement.

He then pointed with the gavel at Mr 'Deer Stalker Hat'. "Sir, please stand up and what is your name?"

"Michael Courtney-Brown your Honour he was struggling to his feet as he said it.

The Magistrate was looking down at the desk and shuffling some papers about "Yes, yes so we understand ... and Mr Courtney-Brown, we think you are responsible for this total waste of time by this Court and the Police, we will be referring this matter to see if there is a case to be brought against you to recover the cost."

My Friend Henry

Turning to me again he had a smile on his lips as he said "We do not wish to delay you further. The Court has one more request and that is for you to make a statement to the Police of what exactly took place on Friday evening. We also make it clear if you wish to take further action to recover any costs you have been incurred in then this Court will not stand in your way." As he said it, he glared at the Police Sergeant.

He lifted up his gavel and hit the desk to finalise the matter. Everyone in the Court room got to their feet and immediately the three justices rose and disappeared into a doorway behind them.

Chapter Twenty Seven

A Double Shock

It was with great relief flowing through me as I walked from the Court Room holding my head high and grinning with my heart beating fast. My little Solicitor joined me and murmured "A good result" as if he had something to do with it. But then again if he had not been there to represent me the result might have been different, as I am sure something went on behind the scenes.

After some quick welcome refreshments in the busy little Café opposite, I returned and he accompanied me to a small room next to the Court building, where it was arranged so that I could give the statement the magistrates had asked me to provide.

It was a lengthy procedure as the Policemen taking it down in long hand would repeat everything I said, first trying to modify the wording, I was too wound up by the whole episode to allow him to do that.

After which when I finally signed the document it was early afternoon. I retrieved the car from the police yard and followed instructions from one of the policemen to a Dealership where I arranged to have the damaged radiator replaced. They promised to carry out

My Friend Henry

the work that afternoon, which was as good a result as possible. I thought I would be able to drive home that evening.

After a struggle to get through on the telephone I finally spoke to my Manager again and explained events, he seemed a lot happier than he did on Saturday morning.

He told me not to worry about the damage to the gate as the company would make an insurance claim as soon as they had the figures to replace it to hand. He then told me to get back as soon as possible. Before ringing off he had a nag about personal telephone calls going to the office as a lady had called me a few times. I thought it was probably Sally.

I called into the Garage to see how the work was going only to be told they could not obtain a replacement for the damaged part saying hopefully they would have one the following day. I found a small hotel and booked in for the night. After that it was time to have a proper meal, after a stroll around I found in the centre of the town a reasonably sized restaurant.

The displayed menu outside in a frame looked acceptable if not exciting. It was busy inside which was reassuring

My Friend Henry

and it was also more comfortable than the exterior gave the impression of. A waiter showed me to a table and after taking my order he provided me with the morning newspaper to read while I waited to be served.

I flipped through the pages not really interested in what was written, still smiling to myself at the events of the morning. Although disappointed at the events on Friday afternoon and the loss of what was going to be a wonderful weekend.

I was relaxed and comfortable with how things had turned out. I was calculating in my head the cost of the last few days and the amount to claim against the Police and the man with the deer stalker hat. When the heading on one of the stories, tucked away on one of the inner pages caught my eye as the word Palmer jumped out at me.

I almost smiled at it and then with a shock on reading the article, which stated Professor Palmer who had been sixty, had been killed in an accident on an Oil Rig in South Africa. The part that really took my attention was when it stated that his wife was expecting their first child which was due in June.

My Friend Henry

The meal arrived and it looked more pleasant than the menu suggested. I was chewing a piece of savoury meat and reminiscing of the clandestine times Mrs Palmer and I had spent together and how she often had said 'don't worry you cannot make me pregnant.'

I carried on with the meal although in the back of my mind I was calculating nine months back from June. Suddenly, I stopped eating with shock. I had remembered it was the period last year when her husband had been away in the Far East for a lengthy period starting from that August.

I swallowed hard. Thinking back to those months when we had seen a lot of each other. Was it possible the baby was mine? But then I had seen her with another man, but that was a lot later around Christmas time and that is only six months before June. I then had another thought, who was the female telephoning me at the car site, could it be Mrs Palmer?

Chapter Twenty Eight

Back to Work

The garage was having difficulty in obtaining a new radiator because the car was a new model and spares for it were not readily available or easy to get hold of, so it was not until late on the Wednesday morning was I able to make my way back to London.

I drove straight to the car site hoping to make my peace with my boss. He smiled and told me to get back to work saying something like these things happen. Julie passed me a note as if it was top secret murmuring it is from your girlfriend in a huffy sort of way. I opened the folded piece of paper hoping to see some words from Sally ... it wasn't from her but Mrs Palmer. Very brief just asking for me to call her.

I slipped it in my pocket, not understanding my own feelings as it had now been five days since I last saw Sally and as each moment passed, I dearly wanted to speak to her. The thought of speaking to Mrs Palmer was furthest from my mind as I could not wait until the end of the working day to make contact with Sally, all the time wondering why she had not called. However, I had made it clear in our early relationship not to call the office as it was not liked.

My Friend Henry

During a brief lull in events I managed to use the phone to call Sally's office only to be told they had not seen her since last Friday when I had called in to collect her and they had not heard from her. That set my heart beating and instead of hearing her soft gentle voice, nothing, but disappointment.

I instantly recognised the car as it entered the car site, it was a distinct Cortina dissimilar to the norm as the paint work was different with a green flash down the side. I remembered the specification of it clearly when I had sold the car to the Palmers and their requirement of wanting something unique.

She stepped out of the car looking as lovely as usual although a little plump around the waist where baby was growing, although if you didn't know about the child she looked quite normal.

Those flashing eyes bore into me like twin daggers as she demanded if I had been trying to avoid her. My excuse of being away for a few days sounded a bit lame, and then quickly added "The management do not like personal callers so let us walk around looking at cars as if you wanted to part exchange your existing one." As I said it I was walking round the Cortina as if studying for damage or just plain wear.

My Friend Henry

She looked at me as if I was mad. I smiled at her and said, "I like working here and I would prefer to continue doing so ... so please humour me and let us walk around some cars, so management think I am at least trying to do my job?"

Mrs Palmer didn't quite laugh but almost, she looked me up and down for the moment as if I didn't exist. She turned and did what I suggested and wandered over to a two seater convertible and even opened the door as if she was interested.

I was tongue tied, what was I supposed to say to her? Nevertheless, making a start by saying "I was sorry to hear about your husband." A tear glistened in her eyes and she looked away and studied the car.

My heart went out to her, she was different as she was no longer flaunting her body, instead she seemed lost and vulnerable. We both felt like strangers struggling to find words and disorientated in the cruel turn of events. I found myself saying "Look this is not the place to talk ... why don't we arrange to meet later?"

She looked up at me and smiled "Yes. You are right I should not have come here. Would you please call me? I was nodding my head when over her shoulder I saw

My Friend Henry

Eileen's Jaguar pull up at the kerb side. I felt uncomfortable as if I was under attack.

While encouraging Mrs. Palmer to go back to her car I saw Eileen getting out of hers. It was at that moment Julie came up to me and told me I was wanted in the office.

The call to the office was of no consequence and I had a feeling it was a ruse to get me away from Mrs Palmer as it must have been obvious, she was not here to buy a car.

It was not unusual for Eileen to be at the car site as she often did some work for the Company which needed legal advice, in any case that was where I first met her when, all that time ago she had returned some documents.

As I watched Eileen in her day attire of a smart navy blue business suit with her high heels clip clopping over the paved area, which made her look sexier than in some of her more revealing outfits.

Suddenly I realised it was Wednesday and our usual evening get together, and I had compromised it by promising to get in touch with Mrs Palmer later. It did not help as Eileen walked past me she winked and said

My Friend Henry

"See you at seven for something special." Which set me wondering what something 'special' could be. I watched as brief case in hand she went through the main doors of the main office building.

Chapter Twenty Nine

Dad! To be?

The remainder of the day dragged on and by missing my lunch break I could be on my way at four o'clock. First stop Sally's house. I was certain because her firm had not heard from her, she must be unwell.

As I pulled up outside the semi detached property I had a feeling it was empty, somehow it had a derelict look. Nonetheless, I almost sprinted up the path and after

My Friend Henry

ringing the bell waited patiently at the closed door for some reply.

In the past I had noticed the elderly lady who lived next door; she would come out for some reason or another and glare at me before disappearing where she had come from.

She did not let me down. There was a click as she opened her front door and she appeared with her pinny to the fore and as usual wiping her hands on it and looking at me as if I was trespassing. "No use knocking on that door, they have gone away."

Oh I was stunned and looked at her as if it was her fault but managed to stutter "Where have they gone?"

She shrugged her shoulders and gazed up the street as if she was expecting someone to appear. "How would I know...it is nothing to do with me." Emphasizing the 'me.'

Again, she looked around her as if there were spies waiting to pounce. She moved a little closer and again quickly peering each way and in a lower voice said. "Their girl came home late last Friday evening and there was a terrible row." A quick glance over her shoulder before

My Friend Henry

continuing, "The following morning she was bundled into a car and they were gone and haven't been back since."

I found myself looking up and down the street not knowing what for, so I asked, "Do you know where they were going?"

She glared at me as if I had done something terrible, raising her voice and speaking sharply "How am I to know it is none of my business ... but one thing is certain they won't be back." She said it as if she had scored a point. I looked at my informer expecting more and when it did not happen I tried to prompt her "Oh, and why would that be?" I was smiling trying to reassure her.

Once more she was looking around her and I could not help letting my eyes follow the same direction. She returned and stared at me in the eyes as if to judge my reaction "Because the removal people arrived on Monday morning and removed their belongings."

I was in shock. My secret agent looked me up and down again with a smirk on her lined face and holding her head up she returned through the door and shut it with a click.

My Friend Henry

I stood looking at the empty house remembering the times I had stood there with my heart beating knowing Sally would come into view very shortly. I wanted to wait there until she appeared but with a heavy heart I trudged back to the car and sat in it for a while still hoping the neighbour was wrong.

'Why should she be?' I asked myself. I had a feeling I had lost the only lady I wanted to be with, and I had a feeling I would never see that beautiful smile again.
Fifteen minutes later I was at another door and another house. This time it was Mrs Palmers. Again, I remembered the times I had stood there with a song in my heart and fantastic anticipation.

This time it was very different, shortly after the door chimes finished she was standing there, dressed tidily but nothing like I was used to seeing on previous occasions. There was not much of a greeting when she said "I thought you were going to phone first?" she turned leaving the door open for me to follow.

The first thing I noticed was the absence of any picture of the husband. The second was her attitude not one of welcome as she sat down without acknowledging I was standing close by. Without the normal invitation I took it on myself to sit opposite her on the facing settee. I opened the conversation "I am sorry to hear about Mr Palmer."

She looked up at me with anger on her face and I could see she had been crying. "Don't be! Not for that bastard."

I was taken by surprise by the venom in her voice. "He couldn't wait to get me into bed, and then persuaded me to marry him ... and then the bastard would pretend we were trying for a family, I was so excited and loved him for it ... but the bastard had had an operation ... an operation long before we were married so despite his promises he knew damn well he could not make me pregnant."

Although the child she was carrying was hardly showing she was rubbing her stomach as if reassuring herself it was true there was a baby there. "He was a misery and difficult to live with and as far as he was concerned, I was of little consequence only here for his pleasure."

She gave a little laugh "When I discovered by chance, he could not give me what I so desired, I thought I could be just as deceitful as him and that is when you came into my life."

My Friend Henry

She smiled and looked at me in a different light than the previous few minutes before continuing "The day I first saw you I knew you were the one ... and as they say, the rest is history." She was still smiling and shrugged her shoulders as she said it and it did not matter.

I was stunned to think she had designed the event, and it suddenly came to me, if she planned all that then the next thing will be for me to be here and play Dad. In the back of my mind I was thinking I don't really need this as I was still thinking of where Sally could be. By way of making conversation I asked "Is there something I can do?"

She shook her head and looked up into my face the smile spreading from her eyes and the corners of her mouth lifted as if she had just come to a decision. "Nothing, no nothing at all Dennis. Just stay as a friend ... no more."

She stopped and wiped a tear from her eye. "We could not live together, anyway it would not be right a wife who had just lost her husband taking in a boyfriend to replace him ... anyway, we would end up fighting."

She turned and looked out at the garden as if she was making certain it was still there and then added sadly as if she if did not believe it "I have got everything I

My Friend Henry

want and I will enjoy being a widow and bringing up the little one who will always remind me of you. In any case I have my family who will help to take care of me." Turning she poured two glasses of Scotch and handing me one she said "Cheers, for old time's sake and the fun we had together."

A short time later I was ushered out of the front door. I looked back she was still standing there, and I blew her a kiss, which Mrs Palmer responded to as she shut the door.

Chapter Thirty

The Special

I reluctantly went home feeling very low as I felt I had taken advantage of her and had let her down, although I knew she was right we could not have lived together, remembering on a number of occasions when we had not been very compatible and had disagreements, which had become more frequent. I suppose mainly because our upbringing had been totally different. I could not help wondering what Eileen wanted and what she had meant by 'special'.

Automatically pulling up outside Eileen's house I was still trying to work out the puzzle of what had happened to Sally and was a little astounded when my date for the evening, as she usually did, came to the door.

I think she must stand at the window waiting for me to arrive as she had never missed; anyway I was surprised because instead of one of her outfits she 'nearly puts on' she was dressed in long trousers and a frilly top with a small jacket, I wondered briefly if that was the 'special'.

My Friend Henry

I approached the door with a little flutter in the tummy, and as I reached it the familiar smell of her perfume surrounded me. Eileen took hold of my hand squeezing it and gave me a peck on the cheek before leading me into the drawing room, which in my ignorance, we lower down the ladder would call the front room.

It was a nice airy space, very feminine in decor with a pleasant smell the same or at least matching what she was wearing. On a side table was my favourite tipple, it suddenly struck me the way others poured me a drink as if it was some form of ritual which I needed on a regular basis.

Eileen picked up a Gin and Tonic, pink of course, and sat down opposite me, crossing her legs demurely as if I had never seen them before, watching her action I felt Henry taking notice, that was down to my memory.

We looked at each other sipping our drinks and me wondering what was going to happen next. I smiled saying "This is very pleasant." She smiled back at me. I had been in the room before but not with just the two of us, on those occasions it had been when she had held a house party for close friends, in those days we had been seen as a couple and normally I would stay the night.

My Friend Henry

As time drifted past I could not help feeling a funny atmosphere, something unusual, she seemed to be thinking and then looked down at her drink, "Last week I was busy modifying a contract for one of my clients." She looked up at me and smiled. She had seemed to have hesitated or perhaps stopped, so I prompted with the one word "And?"

Turning her gaze and looking out of the window as if I was not there and fiddling with her glass before continuing "Works for a large Japanese Organisation." My heart fluttered, so did Sally's father. I waited.

"Some time ago he was offered a new post in the Channel Islands, which he had been putting off taking. Suddenly last week he decided to take up the offer, which is the reason why I got involved because it meant a change in the wording on his contract ... enough of that I thought for a change we could go and see a film this evening, it is a new block buster."

My mouth had gone dry, I took another sip of the drink and looked at her saying "I think I would like to stay here and hear more about the Channel Islands?"

My Friend Henry

"There is not a lot more to say except I don't think it is the largest of the group ... and at that I have said too much." She was still smiling and totally relaxed looking at me as if I was something special. "I have two tickets for a matinee this evening ... it's for a film which will be released shortly ... care to go?"

I remembered in the past she would be offered tickets before a film was released although she had never given me the chance to go with her before. I nodded my head and now I knew why she had dressed differently than on previous occasions.

"Sounds good, will we have time to eat somewhere first?" Assessing to myself that perhaps she would tell me more about the Channel Islands.

It turned out to be a fun evening different from most with Eileen who was a 'hotch potch' of diverse attitudes and mood swings from the very serious to a take off of a giggling teenager. Although I hinted during the evening of wanting more detail about her earlier statement nothing more was coming. I knew in my heart she had already said too much and was feeling guilty for broadcasting client confidentiality.

My Friend Henry

After the picture show I dropped her off at her house where we exchanged pleasantries. I made my way home puzzling about what she and the neighbour had said and came to the conclusion Sally was with her parents and was now living in the Channel Islands. But what could I do about it?

Chapter Thirty One

Despair

After a very bad night's sleep, I was still feeling very low as I dragged myself out of the bed the following morning, and after the normal routine of something to eat and in a sombre mood after a poor eight hours rest, I made my way to the car site where I tried to be bright and breezy. It was not possible, less than a week ago I was with the love of my life and looking forward to the future with her and now, nothing.

The depression hit me hard and my brain kept drifting to that group of Islands off the French coast. It was a strange feeling, as if the past few days had not happened and shortly I would be seeing Sally.

On a number of occasions, I would see a woman with similar hair style and my heart would leap in anticipation only to be disappointed. My big concern, it was many months until my holiday period so it would be some time before I could get away and try and find the one person I wanted to be with.

The days dragged on and I realised my mind was not coping with the commerce part of the job, selling cars,

My Friend Henry

as I was not responding very well also my colleagues were starting to comment. It was a couple of weeks later when one day a bolshie couple with their group of children came on the site and started looking at various cars.

I approached them and went into the normal routine of what they were looking for and did they have a car to part exchange. The woman was poorly dressed with no makeup and seemed very timid as she dragged herself along behind her husband, while the kids were ignored and did exactly what they wanted, climbing in and out of vehicles at will.

The husband was a big man, not very well dressed in a tee shirt and scruffy trainers and he marched around and in a loud voice telling me and his wife the good and bad things about the various models.

Whilst he was busy telling the world what his thoughts were and being totally negative about everything and ignoring me most of the time, the children continued running around screaming or being just generally noisy.

I felt my patience was getting short as it was difficult to have a meaningful conversation with the 'know all' who would contradict anything and everything I said.

My Friend Henry

A few weeks before I would have laughed it off and with time changed his attitude. However, my head was buzzing trying to keep an eye on what their off springs were doing and following them around wondering where and what he was going to criticise next.

It came to a head when one of the kids started to try and undo one of the wiper blades on a car saying something like "Hi Dad! You need a new wiper blade how about this one?" His father retorted "Great idea they are a load of thieves, so they won't miss it!"

Something snapped inside me and I told them what I thought of them and to get off the site. The one good thing about my outburst was I did not swear which would have meant instant dismissal. Instead what happened? I got a dressing down by management, who in their wisdom recognised I was not my normal self and told me to take a couple of weeks off to get over my problems.

It is funny how some things happen as if by design for when I got home that afternoon laying on the doormat a white envelope with just my Christian name typed on the cover.

My Friend Henry

I was intrigued and turned it over in my hand. Before opening it I slipped out of my jacket and went into the living room (front room) laying the coat across a chair. Standing in front of the window I looked at it once more and with my heart beating faster it was time to see inside it.

I soon as I slit the envelope open, I smelt that familiar perfume, the one that Eileen always wore, it was as if she was there in person. No message just one typed line spelling out an address in Guernsey in the Channel Islands.

Now I realised why she had not seen me since the evening of the cinema, she had wanted to tell me and she could not do that in person.

Eileen, the professional solicitor had found another way, without feeling embarrassed about declaring a client's confidences, and by now no doubt had put her action out of her clever mind, it also explained why the evening had been special. I was elated and wanted to phone her to thank her, but knew if I did she would be annoyed and would not appreciate it.

Chapter Thirty Two

The Little Car

I did not own a car as I always had the option of having one of the vehicles we were selling for personal use, now it was a problem how to go to the address in the envelope. I had a choice of either flying to Guernsey or hiring a car and going by boat. I chose the latter and spoilt myself with a roomy little two seater, which was fun to drive but being low down in the seat it was a little daunting in traffic looking up at the other vehicles.

The drive down to Portsmouth was uneventful and I was there in plenty of time to catch the Ferry for the six and half hour crossing to the Island.

I was excited and yet I was feeling a little foolish, supposing she did not want to see me when I got there. There was also the fact that maybe she wasn't there, maybe she lived and loved elsewhere, for I knew nothing other than an address where they had moved to six weeks previously.

I drove off the Ferry in the late afternoon turning left and left again to exit the port. First thing was to find a hotel and then a road map of the island, forty minutes

My Friend Henry

later I had achieved both objectives. It was then that I regretted the choice of motor car as it was too outstanding and noticeable, it was not something you could drive past without creating attention. But why should I worry about that?

I had the hood down on the car early the following morning just after eight, the sun was warm and bright, the airstream was ruffling my hair as I went in search of the address. It turned out to be in the old part of the town, quaint little terraced houses on a road with an incline away from the harbour.

I drove slowly up to it squinting over the windscreen looking for the number I wanted. I was surprised as nearer the top of the road the houses were more modern, one of which laid back from the road with the number proudly displayed on the wall by the gate in the numerals I wanted.

I stopped the car a little way past it and sat looking back at the gate through the driving mirrors and contemplating what to do next. All sorts of mad schemes came into my head from delivering flowers to being a window cleaner.

My Friend Henry

It was just before nine o'clock when a black saloon car pulled up outside the house and I watched as Sally's father and her brother came out through the gate. The elder had a brief case in his hand and they both climbed into the back of the waiting vehicle. I watched as the car changed direction to the one it had come from and drove away.

I put the car in gear and went a little way up the road and turned the car around and stopped on the opposite side of the road where I had been before, this time facing down the hill. My heart was racing with various feelings chasing through me, one which had nagged at me for the past few weeks was why had she not been in touch? Why had she not written? It was these thoughts that were preventing me from running up to the door to find her.

The sun was starting to burn the back of my neck. I got out of the car and was wrestling with the canvas hood and trying to erect it. Another car was coming up the hill this time a taxi, it came to a halt outside the house and the driver blew the horn.

I don't know why but I stood beside the car mesmerised. Perhaps an inner feeling told me to be recognised.

My Friend Henry

I heard the sound of familiar footsteps and into view the more familiar shape of Sally in a dark business suit with a white blouse and her blond hair flowing in the wind.

She was about to reach for the door handle of the taxi when she looked up over the car and our eyes met.

The thrill of that unforgettable moment flooded through me. She must have had similar thoughts as she froze and looked at me in astonishment.

Sally did a little dance and walked quickly towards me her face lighting up as the smile spread across it.

We fell into each other's arms she was murmuring "What are you doing here?"

It was a simple answer "I have come to fetch you ... there is a quaint little cottage by the sea still waiting for us."

She looked at me nodding her head and eyes wide and sparkling. With excitement in her voice Sally said, "Do you mean now?"

My Friend Henry

At that moment the taxi driver came over and said, "Look Miss, I aint got all day, are you coming or not?"

She didn't even look at him her eyes still smiling into mine as she said "I'm not going to need you now." Then he made a demand for his fare I took a note out of my wallet which satisfied him, and he drove away.

It was a great feeling as she naturally slid into the small seat next to me. We briefly held hands and smiled at each other. Then it was time to start our life together.

I slid the car into gear and the two of us followed the direction the other car had taken, down the hill and into the future both feeling contented and relaxed with each other's company in the little car.

My Friend Henry

Percy with three of his five awards

Percy W. Chattey's first thrilling novel was published in 1984 after which he concentrated on his Architectural Design Practice and did not start writing again until he retired in two thousand and twelve. During the following six years he has published ten full length novels, five of them have won first place in their own genre in the American 'Pinnacle Awards'

Percy also publishes on a by-monthly basis the 'Story Telling Series' which are one hundred and twenty page booklets of short stories, some funny others interesting, also on a regular basis the

My Friend Henry

history of well known names. At the time of writing (2018) nine of these booklets have been published. This is the tenth in the series.

My Friend Henry

The 'Story Telling' Series is published by
Percychatteybooks.

<u>Percychatteybooks</u>
Story Telling©
Somerset House
6070 Birmingham Business Park
Birmingham
B37 7BF
Registered Number 2299335

My Friend Henry, comprised
written and published in the Hondon Valley, Spain